TRAPPED WITH THE FOREST RANGER

ANGEL'S PEAK

ELLIE MASTERS

MASTER OF ROMANTIC SUSPENSE

JEM PUBLISHING

DEDICATION

This book is dedicated to my one and only—my amazing and wonderful husband.

Without your care and support, my writing would not have made it this far.

You pushed me when I needed to be pushed.

You supported me when I felt discouraged.

You believed in me when I didn't believe in myself.

If it weren't for you, this book never would have come to life.

Also by Ellie Masters

The LIGHTER SIDE

Ellie Masters is the lighter side of the Jet & Ellie Masters writing duo! You will find Contemporary Romance, Military Romance, Romantic Suspense, Billionaire Romance, and Rock Star Romance in Ellie's Works.

YOU CAN FIND ELLIE'S BOOKS HERE:

ELLIEMASTERS.COM/BOOKS

SUGGESTED READING ORDER

START HERE

Rockstar Romance

The Angel Fire Rock Romance Series

EACH BOOK IN THIS SERIES CAN BE READ AS A STANDALONE AND IS ABOUT A DIFFERENT COUPLE WITH AN HEA.

IT IS RECOMMENDED THEY ARE READ IN ORDER.

Heart's Insanity

Ashes to New

Heart's Desire

Heart's Collide

Hearts Divided

Hearts Entwined

Forest's FALL

Hearts The Last Beat

CONTINUE HERE...

Rescuing Malia

Rescuing Ally (Part 1)

Rescuing Ally (Part 2)

Delta Team

Rescuing Ember

Rescuing Aria

STANDALONES IN THE GUARDIAN HOSTAGE RESCUE SERIES YOU CAN READ ANYTIME

Military Romance

Guardian Personal Protection Specialists

Sybil's Protector

Lyra's Protector

Angel's Peak Series

Steamy Instalove Small Town

EACH BOOK IN THIS SERIES CAN BE READ AS A STANDALONE AND IS ABOUT A DIFFERENT COUPLE WITH AN HEA.

SNOWED IN WITH THE MOUNTAIN DOCTOR

Rescued by the Mountain Guide

Stranded with the Resort Owner

Matched with the Small-Town Chef

Trapped with the Forest Ranger

Snowbound with the Vineyard Owner

Reunited with the Hometown Hero

Colliding with the Coffee Shop Owner

Falling for the Firefighter

Wrecked with the Reclusive Author

Tangled with the Single Dad

Whirlwinded by the Helicopter Pilot

Sheltered by the Veterinarian

Bound by the Sheriff

The One I Want Series

(Small Town, Military Heroes)

By Jet & Ellie Masters

EACH BOOK IN THIS SERIES CAN BE READ AS A STANDALONE
AND IS ABOUT A DIFFERENT COUPLE WITH AN HEA.

Saving Abby

Saving Ariel

Saving Brie

Saving Cate

Saving Dani

Saving Jen

The LaRouge Triplets

Asher

Brody

Cage

Billionaire Romance

Billionaire Boys Club

Hawke

Richard

Contemporary Romance

Cocky Captain

Romantic Suspense

Each book is a standalone novel.

The Starling

The Swan

~AND~

Science Fiction

Ellie Masters writing as L.A. Warren

Vendel Rising: a Science Fiction Serialized Novel

If you enjoyed this book by Ellie Masters, the LIGHTER SIDE of the Jet & Ellie writing duo, and aren't afraid of edgier writing, you might enjoy reading BDSM themed books written by Jet, the DARKER SIDE of the Masters' Writing Team.

The DARKER SIDE

Jet Masters is the darker side of the Jet & Ellie writing duo!

Romantic Suspense

Changing Roles Series:

This series must be read in order.

Command Me

Control Me

Collar Me

Embracing FATE

Seizing FATE

Accepting FATE

HOT READS

To My Readers

This book is a work of fiction. It does not exist in the real world and should not be construed as reality. As in most romantic fiction, I've taken liberties. I've compressed the romance into a sliver of time. I've allowed these characters to develop strong bonds of trust over a matter of days.

This does not happen in real life where you, my amazing readers, live. Take more time in your romance and learn who you're giving a piece of your heart to. I urge you to move with caution. Always protect yourself.

Angel's Peak

Grab the First Book in The Guardian Hostage Rescue Specialists Series for Free

https://elliemasters.com/RescuingMelissa

Angel's Peak

Chapter 1

THE GOLDEN EAGLE SOARS ABOVE THE RIDGE, majestic wings spread against the backdrop of Angel's Peak. My breath catches in my throat as I raise my camera, adjusting the telephoto lens with trembling fingers. After three days of hiking, countless mosquito bites, and one terrifying encounter with a mother bear and her cubs, this moment makes every hardship worth it.

"Just a little closer," I whisper.

The magnificent bird banks left, sunlight gleaming off its distinctive plumage. I track its movement, heart pounding with the thrill of the chase. The perfect shot waits, suspended in the moment between breath and release.

Click. Not quite right. *Click*. Too distant. *Click*. Almost...

Dark clouds gather on the horizon, rolling over the mountaintops like a tide of smoke. I've been watching them approach for the past hour, calculating how much time I have before the storm hits. Not enough, according to the sensible part of my brain. Plenty, insists the photographer in me who's been chasing this eagle for my father's unfinished collection.

The wind shifts, carrying the scent of rain and ozone-never

good. The eagle circles higher, moving farther from my position.

"Don't you dare leave." I edge closer to the outcropping, ignoring the first heavy drops that spatter against my jacket sleeve.

A low rumble of thunder echoes through the valley, vibrating in my chest. The rational voice grows louder, urging me to pack up and seek shelter.

I've been in mountain storms before.

They move fast and hit hard, especially in this part of Colorado.

But Dad never gave up on the perfect shot.

The eagle makes one more sweeping arc, golden feathers catching a final ray of sunlight before the clouds swallow the sky. My finger hovers over the shutter—

Lightning splits the darkened sky, followed instantly by a crack of thunder that nearly sends me stumbling backward. The eagle vanishes, a speck disappearing into the tumultuous clouds.

"Dammit!"

Rain comes suddenly, not in drops but sheets. Within seconds, my equipment is drenched. I scramble to pack my camera into its waterproof case, but my rain cover flaps uselessly in the wind, torn from my backpack by the force of the gale.

Water streams down my face, into my eyes, soaking through layers meant to protect against light showers, not biblical floods. I abandon the tripod, cradling my camera bag against my chest as I scan the ridge for shelter.

The storm transforms familiar terrain into an alien landscape. Trails become muddy rivulets. Visibility drops to mere feet. Another lightning strike illuminates a dense copse of trees to my right. Not ideal for lightning, but better than standing exposed on the ridge.

My boots slip on rain-slicked stone as I half-run, half-slide down the slope toward the tree line. One misstep sends me sprawling, my knee colliding with a jagged rock. Pain lances through my leg, but adrenaline keeps me moving.

The relative cover of pine boughs offers little respite. Water finds its way through the canopy, soaking me further. Lightning illuminates the valley again, closer this time, followed immediately by a thunderclap that drowns out my curse.

Through the curtain of rain, I spot something—a structure nestled among the trees further down the slope. A cabin? A shed? At this point, even a damn outhouse would be welcome.

I clutch my camera bag tighter and push forward, ignoring the throbbing in my knee. Each step becomes a negotiation with mud and gravity. The wind whips my face with wet strands of hair that have rebelliously escaped from my once-secure ponytail.

As I draw closer, the building's shape solidifies. A ranger station, judging by the forest service logo visible even through the downpour. Relief floods through me stronger than the storm. Civilization. Shelter. Maybe even a first aid kit for my bleeding knee.

The wooden steps creak beneath my weight as I climb to the covered porch. Rain drums against the roof, a deafening percussion that almost drowns out my pounding on the door. Lightning flares again, illuminating the station's windows— warm light glows from within. Someone's home.

I bang harder, desperation lending strength to my fist.

The door swings open with such sudden force that I stumble inward and straight into the arms of a man. Tall and broad-shouldered, his expression is as thunderous as the sky. Dark hair falls across his forehead, nearly touching eyebrows drawn together in annoyance and surprise. His jaw—covered with at least three days of stubble—clenches as he takes in my bedraggled appearance.

"Station's closed to visitors." His voice is low, graveled, like he doesn't use it often.

"I'm not a visitor." Water streams from my hair, pooling at my feet. "I'm a half-drowned photographer who's about to lose ten thousand dollars worth of equipment if I don't get out of this storm."

Another lightning strike punctuates my statement, close enough that the subsequent thunder rattles the windows. The man's gaze flicks from my face to my camera bag, then to the storm raging behind me.

That's when our eyes truly meet, and something unexpected jolts through me. His eyes are the color of forest moss after rain, deep green with flecks of amber. They widen slightly, an almost imperceptible reaction that sends a strange heat through my chilled body.

"Please." The word escapes without permission, embarrassingly close to begging.

He steps back from the doorway, a reluctant invitation. "You're tracking mud."

Not "come in" or "let me help you." Just an observation about the trail of muck following me into his pristine domain. Charming.

"Stellar observation skills. Must be why they made you a ranger." I clutch my camera bag closer, water dripping from my elbows onto his wooden floor.

The door closes behind me with a decisive click, sealing out the chaos of the storm. The cabin's warmth wraps around me, highlighting just how thoroughly soaked and frozen I've become. My teeth chatter as I stand awkwardly in the entryway, uncertain of my welcome despite being inside.

"Stay there." He points to a small mat by the door. "I'll get towels."

Left alone, I take in my surroundings. The station is smaller than it appeared from outside—a single room with a kitchenette in one corner, a desk covered in maps and logbooks in another, and a small sitting area centered around a currently dormant woodstove. A door presumably leads to sleeping quarters. Every surface gleams with meticulous care. No personal touches adorn the walls, just official forest service maps and wildlife identification charts.

The ranger returns with a stack of towels, thrusting them toward me with minimal eye contact.

"Thank you..." I trail off, realizing I don't know his name.

"Caleb." He offers nothing more, watching as I set my camera bag carefully on the bench by the door before taking the towels.

"Harper Wells." I wrap one towel around my shoulders and use another to blot my dripping hair. "Wildlife photographer. I was tracking a golden eagle when the storm hit."

His only response is a noncommittal grunt as he moves to the kitchenette, filling a kettle with water. The silence stretches uncomfortably as I dry myself as best I can, hyperaware of the puddle forming beneath me despite my efforts.

"Your knee is bleeding."

I glance down at the torn fabric of my hiking pants, the smear of blood visible through the rip. "Fell on the way down." I shrug, trying to project nonchalance rather than the pain throbbing with each heartbeat.

Caleb disappears again, returning with a small first aid kit. He points to a chair at the small table. "Sit."

"I can handle it."

"Sit." The single word holds no room for argument.

I lower myself gingerly onto the wooden chair, wincing as I extend my injured leg. Caleb kneels before me, his movements economical as he opens the kit. His proximity sends an inexplicable wave of awareness through me—the scent of pine and woodsmoke clinging to his flannel shirt, the careful precision of his large hands.

"This will sting." His warning comes a second before alcohol meets raw flesh.

I hiss through clenched teeth, fingers gripping the edge of the chair. "Thanks for the heads-up."

The ghost of a smile touches his lips before vanishing so quickly I wonder if I imagined it. He works in silence, cleaning the wound. His fingers are calloused but gentle, a contradiction that draws my attention more than it should.

"Not too deep." He applies antiseptic ointment and covers the cut with a bandage. "No stitches needed."

"Good. I left my suture kit in my other pants."

This time, the slight twitch of his lips is definitely real. Victory.

The kettle whistles, saving him from having to respond. He rises in one fluid motion, returning to the kitchenette. I watch as he prepares two mugs of tea, his broad back turned to me. The storm continues its assault, rain lashing against windows, wind howling through the surrounding forest while I check out how amazing those pants make his ass look.

"Sugar?" He doesn't turn around.

"No, thanks. Plain is fine."

He returns with the tea, placing one mug before me before retreating to lean against the counter, maintaining distance between us. The warm ceramic feels heavenly against my cold fingers.

"So, Ranger Caleb, do you always welcome storm-stranded photographers with such enthusiasm, or am I special?"

His eyes narrow slightly. "Most people check the weather forecast before heading into the backcountry."

"I did check. It said afternoon thunderstorms were possible. It's afternoon. There's a thunderstorm. Forecast accurate."

"Possible means prepare for it, not ignore it until you're caught in it."

I take a sip of tea to avoid responding immediately. He's right, which irritates me. I detest looking like an idiot. I did check the weather, and I may, or may not, have been a bit too eager to get in my shot. I don't like that he's pointing out my foolishness. "I needed that eagle shot. It's part of a collection I'm finishing for my father."

Something in my tone must communicate the deeper meaning, because his expression shifts slightly. Not softening, exactly, but less judgmental.

"Where's your campsite?" he asks after a moment.

"Blue Spruce Campground. About six miles southwest."

He glances out the window at the intensifying storm, then at the radio on his desk. As if on cue, it crackles to life.

"Sierra Station, this is Dispatch. Do you copy?" A woman's voice, distorted by static.

Caleb crosses to the radio. "This is Sierra Station. Go ahead, Dispatch."

"Flash flood warning issued for your area. Palmer Creek has overflowed. Roads to Blue Spruce Campground are washed out. We're evacuating campers via the northern route."

My stomach drops. My rental car, my tent, my supplies— all at Blue Spruce.

"Any timeline on road clearing?" Caleb asks, eyes flicking briefly to me.

"Not yet. Assessment team can't get in until the storm passes. Expecting at least three days before the southern routes are passable. Check in at 0800 tomorrow for updates."

"Copy that. Sierra Station out."

Silence falls as Caleb replaces the radio handset. He turns to face me, expression unreadable.

"Looks like you'll be staying here tonight." His tone suggests this development ranks somewhere between finding a dead mouse in his boot and discovering his coffee supply has run out.

"I can try to hike back another way—"

"No." The word is sharp, brooking no argument. "Night hiking in a flood zone during an electrical storm is suicide."

Lightning flashes again, followed immediately by a thunderous boom that rattles the windows in their frames. We both glance toward the sound.

"Three days," I say softly, the reality sinking in. "They said at least three days."

Caleb's jaw tightens as he looks back at me. "The station has basic supplies. You can take the bed in the back room."

"Where will you sleep?"

"I'll manage." His tone ends the discussion.

Three days trapped with a man who clearly wishes I were anywhere but here. So why can't I stop staring at his hands? Or his ass. Damn those jeans.

Angel's Peak

Chapter 2

Sunlight streams through unfamiliar windows, painting golden rectangles across rough-hewn floorboards. For a moment, disorientation grips me—this isn't my tent. Then yesterday's events flood back: the ranger station and the man with storm-swept eyes. A man whose reluctant hospitality saved me from being washed down the mountainside.

I sit on the narrow bed, wincing as my knee protests the movement. The small back room is spartan—a bed, a simple wooden chest, and a hook on the wall holding a single towel. No personal touches. No indication that a human being sleeps here. Caleb is a particularly tidy ghost.

The cabin beyond the door is silent. I pull on yesterday's still-damp jeans, grimacing at the clammy fabric against my skin, and limp into the main room.

Empty.

The woodstove holds glowing embers, evidence that Caleb has been up for some time. The room is meticulously tidy, no sign of where he might have slept. A folded piece of paper sits on the small dining table with my name scrawled across the top in surprisingly elegant handwriting.

I unfold it, scanning the message:

Harper,

On patrol until midday. Help yourself to coffee and break-fast supplies. Water is limited—5 minute showers max. Don't touch the radio equipment. Stay within sight of the cabin if you go outside.

- C

No "good morning." No, "hope you slept well." Just rules and boundaries as stark as the cabin itself.

"Charming," I mutter to the empty room.

My stomach rumbles, reminding me that my last meal was an energy bar somewhere around noon yesterday. I explore the kitchenette, finding a canister of coffee, oatmeal packets, and a loaf of bread that looks homemade. The refrigerator contains eggs, butter, and a surprising array of fresh vegetables.

I brew coffee and toast a slice of bread, savoring the rich aroma that fills the small space. With food in my stomach and caffeine entering my bloodstream, my natural curiosity takes over.

The cabin invites exploration, not because it's large, but because it feels like a puzzle missing pieces. Who is this man who lives surrounded by wilderness with minimal possessions and apparently no personal life?

The main room contains forest service maps, wildlife iden-tification charts, and bookshelves filled with volumes on ecol-ogy, wilderness survival, and land management. I scan the titles, building a picture of Caleb through his reading habits. A man of science and practical knowledge. No fiction. No poetry. Nothing to suggest he sees the forest as anything but a system to be monitored and maintained.

My gaze falls on a wooden chest tucked beneath the desk. Unlike the rest of the furniture, this piece seems personal—the wood darkened with age and handling, brass fittings tarnished in a way that speaks of years rather than months. I hesitate, my conscience warring with curiosity.

Curiosity wins. Was there any doubt?

I glance toward the door before kneeling beside the chest, wincing as my injured knee protests. The lid opens silently on well-oiled hinges, revealing contents that tell more about Caleb than anything else in the cabin.

A medal, its ribbon slightly frayed, bears the insignia of the Wildland Firefighter Foundation. Several newspaper clippings, yellowed with age, show a younger Caleb in firefighting gear, his face less weathered but his eyes holding the same green of wild places. The headline reads: "Hotshot Crew Saves Twelve in Mountain Blaze."

Beneath these, wrapped in soft cloth, I find a framed photograph. A group of men and women in firefighting uniforms stand arm-in-arm, faces smudged with soot but smiling. Caleb stands at the center, his arm around a woman with curly red hair and a brilliant smile. They look happy. Connected. Nothing like the isolated man who reluctantly sheltered me.

The sound of boots on the porch sends me scrambling, barely managing to close the chest and return to the table before the door swings open.

Caleb fills the doorway, daylight silhouetting his tall frame. His eyes find me immediately, narrowing slightly as if assessing whether I've disturbed his carefully ordered world.

"Morning." I raise my coffee cup in greeting, hoping my face doesn't betray my snooping.

He nods, hanging his jacket on a hook by the door. "Sleep okay?"

"Fine, thanks." I watch as he moves to the kitchenette, his movements efficient and contained. "Any updates on the roads?"

"Still out." He pours himself coffee, keeping his back to me.

The man has a mighty fine ass. Tight and powerful, like he was carved for sin and punishment. Broad back tapering into that perfect V, shoulders wide enough to block the sun. Tree-trunk thighs strain against worn denim, each step a study in raw strength and control. His shirt pulls across muscle, clings in all the right places, and I swear the fabric is working over-time just to hold on.

My gaze drags lower, then back up, heat coiling low in my belly. I lift my hand to swipe at my mouth, only half-jokingly —because I may actually be drooling.

No drool.

I'm cool.

"Another storm system is moving in tonight." He speaks robotically to me. Nothing but the barest bones of conversa-tion. It's almost as if he doesn't know how to carry on an actual conversation. It might explain why he's stationed out here, away from the hiking trails, away from civilization.

"Great." I drum my fingers against the mug, searching for neutral conversation. "So, how long have you been stationed here?"

"Three years." He turns, leaning against the counter rather than joining me at the table.

"You like it? Being alone up here?"

"Yes." His gaze is steady, unreadable.

"Man of many words."

A muscle ticks in his jaw. "Did you need something specific?"

"Just making conversation. It's what normal humans do when sharing space."

"I'm working." He moves to the desk, effectively dismissing me as he opens a logbook.

I bite back a retort, reminding myself that I'm an uninvited guest in his fortress of solitude. Instead, I retrieve my camera from its waterproof case, half-expecting water damage or tech tragedy, but the display blinks to life like a loyal dog. Miraculously intact.

I scroll through the shots from yesterday, thumbing past blurred feathers and hopeful failures until I find them—eagles mid-flight, wings stretched, sunlight streaking across the curve of their spines. Not the shot. Not the holy grail. But enough to justify being stranded in the middle of nowhere with a man who communicates mostly in monosyllables and meaningful grunts.

Behind me, the scrape of a chair and the scratch of Caleb's pen mark the beginning of a long, quiet morning. He's settled at the small desk near the window, filling out some report by hand—of course, he writes by hand—and radiating silent intensity like it's a form of heat.

The hours drift.

Outside, the storm has moved on, but the wind lingers—angry and aimless, rushing through the trees like it's still hunting for something to tear apart. The cabin groans beneath the pressure, wooden beams shifting with age and memory, each creak a reminder of just how alone we are out here. Just how exposed.

Inside, it's warm. Oppressively warm. Or maybe that's just me.

The fire crackles low in the hearth, casting flickering shadows that stretch across the room, but my focus isn't on the flames. It's on him.

I try not to notice the way the sleeves of his thermal hug his biceps, how the fabric strains just enough to hint at the strength beneath. Try not to get caught staring when he leans forward, forearms flexing, veins standing out in stark relief against sun-browned skin. His brows draw together in concentration, and his jaw ticks every time he's thinking hard, like even his face refuses to relax until the problem is solved.

Spoiler alert: I fail. Spectacularly.

I pretend to scroll through photos, flipping through them far too fast to process anything. I jot down a note or two that mean nothing, just to give my hands something to do. But mostly, I watch him.

Out of the corner of my eye.

Through my lashes.

Sometimes, when he's turned away.

I drink him in fully, openly, hungrily.

There's a quiet control to the way he moves. Like his body has learned to conserve energy, to never waste a single breath or motion unless it serves a purpose. When he does move— God help me—it's with the kind of deliberate power that makes my stomach dip and my thighs press tight.

Every flex, every shift, is a reminder of the kind of strength he's holding in check.

And I can't stop imagining what it would feel like to be the reason he loses that control.

I've got a full-blown mental highlight reel playing on loop —Caleb's Greatest Hits before noon. Bending to pick up a pen, I'm 99% sure I dropped just to watch him do it again: good God, that back. Broad and muscled, shifting beneath flannel like some kind of wilderness sin.

Stretching one arm overhead, completely unaware—or worse, entirely aware—of the way his shirt rides up just enough to reveal a sliver of taut, sun-warmed skin and the sharp lines of his hip. A crime against fabric, honestly. Should be illegal.

Pushing back from the table with a low, absent sigh, chest rising slow and deep like he's drawing breath straight from the earth itself. Reverent. Dangerous. Enough to make my thighs clench with the ache of uninvited thoughts I can't unthink.

I make two rounds of coffee just to give myself something else to focus on—burn my tongue both times. Then dig into my emergency protein bar stash, not because I'm hungry, but because I need something—anything—to keep my mouth occupied that isn't him.

Still, the silence isn't as tense as it was yesterday. It's changed. Warmer around the edges. Like the air between us is charged with something low and humming, waiting to strike.

Not quite comfortable. But not cold, either. It feels stretched. Pulled taut by something unspoken. Like anticipation.

Or maybe that's just me.

Probably just me.

But then he glances up.

Catches me watching.

And his gaze holds—just half a second too long, but long enough to wreck me. Long enough for heat to flare in my chest and pool low in my belly, a molten rush that makes it hard to swallow, harder to breathe.

Because maybe it's not just me at all.

I'm a hopeless dreamer, always have been. But this? This is new. These fantasies spinning behind my eyes are not fit for daylight or polite company. They're filthy and vivid and so very specific. I'm not just daydreaming about kissing him under the stars—I'm working on chapter three of Fifty Shades of Mount Me.

Because clearly, my brain has decided this cabin needs less solitude and more sin.

Every time he moves, I imagine what those hands would feel like on me. What that gravel voice would sound like ordering me to my knees. And my imagination? She's not interested in sweet, tentative kisses. She's conjuring a dominant ranger with a filthy mouth and zero patience, using my throat like he owns it. Rough. Possessive. Like he's been holding back so long he doesn't know how not to break me a little.

I shift on the bench, thighs pressing tight, heat slick and undeniable. It's getting hot in here. Or maybe just in my head.

As for Caleb? From the way he's ignored me all morning, I'm starting to think he's forgotten I exist. Forgotten he brought a woman into his sacred, brooding wilderness temple. He moves through the cabin like a shadow—focused, efficient, unaffected—while I sit here cataloging every inch of him like I'm preparing for a final exam on his body.

Scratch that.

I'm devouring him.

Every flex of his forearms, every stretch of flannel across his chest, every controlled inhale and slow exhale. I can practically feel him pressed against me, pinning me down with nothing but the weight of his body and a dark promise in his eyes.

The clock ticks toward late afternoon.

The kettle clicks off.

He doesn't offer tea. I don't ask. We've slipped into this strange rhythm—him pretending I'm not here, me pretending I'm not fantasizing about his cock halfway down my throat while he groans and fists my hair like he can't help himself.

It's not romantic. It's raw. Carnal. Dirty in all the right ways.

Outside, the wind crescendos—wild and unrestrained, as if it's echoing the chaos inside my head.

And then—

CRACK.

A sound like the universe splitting down the middle. A tree limb. A power line. Or maybe just the sky breaking open.

My heart lurches. Caleb's already on his feet.

Angel's Peak

CHAPTER 3

I JOLT UPRIGHT, ADRENALINE KICKING IN BEFORE thought can catch up. Caleb's already moving—fast, precise, like his body registered the threat before the sound even finished echoing. He crosses to the window with long, purposeful strides, muscles flexing beneath his shirt like coiled rope.

"What was that?" I follow him, breath tight, pulse ricocheting.

He points through the fogged glass. "Tree down."

And there it is—downhill, just past the clearing. A massive pine lies uprooted, as if the mountain itself coughed it out. The earth's been torn open, roots twisted and raw, limbs shattered, needles scattered like nature's confetti after some violent celebration. The trunk angles toward the shed, too close for comfort.

"Too close to the water line," Caleb mutters, jaw locked tight.

He's already in motion, grabbing a tool belt, sliding into a canvas jacket, all muscle memory and zero hesitation. At the door, he pauses—just briefly—and looks over his shoulder.

"Coming?"

Two syllables. Not warm. Not a question. Just a flick of authority that wraps around my spine and yanks.

I leap to my feet, snag my coat, and shove my arms through the sleeves, breath already fogging in the cool air because that wasn't a request.

That was a command.

And every unholy, unhinged fantasy I've entertained in this cabin—the ones where he pins me against rough wood and tells me what to do with that voice—just stood up and cheered.

Okay. I may have a problem.

But I follow him into the cold anyway, boots crunching through slush, jacket flapping behind me like I'm chasing something I don't fully understand.

Because even as wind slices across my cheeks and branches creak above us, I'm not thinking about fallen trees.

I'm thinking about the way he said coming.

And how badly I want to be.

The fallen tree sprawls across the path like nature's version of don't even think about it—a massive barricade of gnarled bark and brute defiance. The trunk is easily four feet thick, its surface splintered as if it had been mauled by a myth. It's not just down—it's ruined, torn from the earth like the mountain had a tantrum.

Caleb circles it in silence, steps sure and unhurried, eyes scanning the damage with that low-burn intensity he wears like armor. His presence hums like pressure before a storm— quiet, but charged.

"Ground's too saturated." He kneels, pressing thick fingers into the soft, torn soil around the exposed root ball. "The water line runs through here to the shed. Need to check if it's cracked."

"What can I do?"

He glances up, clearly not expecting the offer. For half a second, something shifts in those eyes—green and stormy and focused squarely on me. The weight of his gaze presses into my skin like a fingerprint. Then he straightens and hands me a flashlight, grip firm and efficient.

"Hold this. Shine it where I'm working."

Roger that, mountain man. Keep the orders coming.

And I do. For the next hour, I become his loyal assistant-slash-human workbench-slash-lust-stricken idiot with a flashlight. I hold things. Fetch things. Brace things. Occasionally, I hand him tools I don't know the name of.

Mostly, though, I stare.

Not obviously. Not in a way that would get me slapped in an HR seminar.

But... oh, I stare.

The way his flannel stretches across his back when he bends over? That shirt has no right doing the Lord's work like that. Every time it rides up, exposing that sliver of taut lower back, I lose another year off my life. His jeans cling to his thighs like sin wrapped in denim, and every shovel drag sends his shoulder blades flexing like some kind of erotic Morse code.

He works in clean, economical movements. No fuss. No wasted effort. Just pure, grounded strength that seems to rise straight from the mountain beneath us. It's quiet except for the scrape of tools and the occasional muttered assessment. Not once does he speak to fill the silence. Not once does he look bored, rushed, or uncertain.

And his hands. God, those hands.

Big and callused and competent. The kind of hands that don't just fix things—they know things. The kind that press in deep and don't flinch at what they find. Every time his fingers curl around a pipe wrench or slide into the dirt, I have to bite the inside of my cheek.

Because I'm not thinking about water lines anymore.

I'm thinking about those hands on my hips. Around my throat. Between my thighs.

And when he leans back on his heels and glances up at me again, jaw shadowed, brow damp, muscles taut beneath sweat-dampened flannel—

I nearly drop the damn flashlight.

And then there's his face.

That sharp, brooding edge carved into his features like it was etched by wind and grit. That stubborn little line between his brows—always furrowed like he's trying to solve some eternal problem—sometimes it softens. Just for a blink. When he's deep in focus, when his whole body is tuned into the work in front of him, it slips. That hard edge melts, and for half a second, he looks... human. Vulnerable, almost.

It undoes me.

I want to reach out, press my thumb to that crease, and smooth it away. Maybe follow it with my lips, to see if the rest of his scowl will follow. Or, if I can steal that softness for myself.

Not that I need to touch him to feel him. His presence fills the space between us like smoke. Like heat. He doesn't talk much, but he doesn't have to. His body speaks in a language older than words—muscle and intent, purpose and restraint. Every movement is its own declaration.

And I'm listening.

Loud. And. Clear.

God help me, I might be in full-blown lust with a human brick wall. One who smells like pine needles, woodsmoke, clean sweat, and something darker. Something rough and inevitable. Like the forest conjured him to prove a point.

"Flashlight," he says, holding out his hand without looking up.

I jolt like I've just been caught mid-orgasm. Because in my

head? I absolutely was. Mouth, hands, hips—every inch of me busy worshipping the mountain god in front of me.

"Right. Sorry." My voice comes out too fast, too breathy, and I shove the flashlight into his palm like it might burn me if I linger. My cheeks blaze.

He doesn't flinch. Doesn't tease. Just takes it, adjusting the angle with those big, capable hands that deserve their own Greek myth. The fingers are all rough grip and precise control —surgeon meets lumberjack—and they know exactly what they're doing.

And I keep watching because I am so far past the point of pretending I'm not.

"Pipe cutter." His hand stretches out again, palm up, commanding and calm. He doesn't even glance at me.

Like he just knows I'll be there.

Like I'm already a part of his rhythm. A tool in his hand. A fixture in his world.

The touch is brief. Our fingers barely graze when I pass it over. But it's enough to light me up from the inside, a static charge crawling up my arm, blooming beneath my skin. My breath catches, traitorous and loud in the quiet.

Oh no. No, no, no. We are not doing the slow-motion, eye-locking, accidental-electric-touch scene from a cheesy rom-com.

Except apparently my body didn't get the memo, because my pulse is doing Olympic-level gymnastics, and my knees are threatening to give out on their own.

And then he does look at me.

Those eyes—God, those eyes—lift to mine. Moss and stormclouds. Hard to read. Harder to look away from. They pin me in place, silent and searching. A pause. A flicker of something unspoken.

Then he turns back to the trench like nothing happened.

But I'm not breathing right. And I can't feel my hands.

And now every fantasy I've had since stepping foot in this cabin—every filthy, dominant, woodsmoke-and-command-laced daydream—is stacking like firewood behind my ribs.

I am so screwed.

"Almost done." He slots the pipe into a fitting with practiced ease, hands steady, sure, like he was born with a wrench in one fist and the wilderness in the other.

"Try the pump switch."

The graze of his fingers from a moment ago is still sizzling on my skin like a phantom touch, but I force my feet to move. I head for the shed, doing everything in my power not to let the whole damn scene scramble my neurons.

My boots crunch over pine needles. The air tastes like wet bark and oncoming rain. When I flip the switch, the pump kicks on with a hum and a satisfying gurgle of water rushing through the pipes—like the mountain itself just exhaled.

"No leaks." I call out, already smiling.

He grunts. That's it. One syllable. No celebration. Meanwhile, I'm three stanzas deep into an internal poem about the way his biceps flexed when he twisted the coupling.

Caleb rises from the trench in one fluid motion. His jeans are soaked, molding to his thighs like second skin—tree-trunk thick, muscular, carved by function, not vanity. There's a smear of dirt across one sharp cheekbone, and the whole damn image is so rugged and feral it short-circuits something vital in my brain.

"You're good at that," I say, gesturing at the fixed pipe like it's a masterpiece and not just, you know, functioning plumbing. "Very... capable."

Brilliant. Because what better compliment than "capable" when your ovaries are doing a synchronized floor routine.

His gaze flickers toward me, unreadable. For half a second, I think—hope—I catch the faintest flush climbing his neck.

But it's gone before I can confirm, swallowed up by that stoic wall he wears like armor.

"Basic maintenance," he mutters, wiping his hands on a rag. "Part of the job."

Of course. Just a man. Doing man things. With man hands. In man pants. Fixing things. Looking like a wilderness-dwelling fever dream brought to life by the sheer force of my suppressed libido.

Totally normal.

We start collecting tools. I follow his lead, pretending not to catalog every brush of muscle beneath damp flannel. The wind shifts as we work, sharp and biting, knifing through the trees. It carries the metallic tang of more rain, mixing with pine and cold soil. Caleb pauses, face tilted to the clouds, jaw tight, reading the sky like it's speaking just to him.

"Another system moving in."

I glance upward, the clouds bruised and hanging low, thick as smoke. "Seems like this mountain makes its own rules."

"It does," he says, and something in his voice softens. Just a shade. Like the storm stirred something awake. "Angel's Peak creates a microclimate. Western slope gets twice the rainfall of the eastern."

I blink. Did I just unlock a hidden bonus level? Caleb, Storm Whisperer edition?

"Well, look at that," I murmur. "A man of weather and few words."

He doesn't answer, just hands me a wrench and brushes past, close enough that the heat of his body trails behind like a promise. And I'm suddenly, painfully aware that I am wet.

Not from the rain.

From wanting him.

From standing too close to a living, breathing contradiction—rough hands and quiet knowledge, brutal strength and gentle restraint.

God help me, I want him to snap. Just once. Just for me.

I open my mouth to tease him, maybe nudge that faint spark of interest into an actual conversation, but a fat raindrop splats square between my eyes.

"Inside." He doesn't wait for my response—just scoops up the remaining tools and jogs toward the cabin, and somehow I'm running after him like we're starring in some rugged outdoorsy rom-com.

Angel's Peak

Chapter 4

By the time we hit the porch, rain is falling in sheets, the kind that turns paths to rivers and jeans to cold denim torture devices. Caleb's already inside, stoking the fire like he's been waiting for the chance to wrestle with logs.

I shake out my jacket, peeling off layers while trying not to ogle him—and failing, again.

There's just something about the way he moves—efficient, grounded. No wasted motion. No unnecessary noise. He doesn't just build a fire. He commands it into existence.

The rough scrape of the log against the hearth, the flare of orange catching dry bark—it's intimate. Primal. Like foreplay in flannel.

I pull out my phone, tapping the screen. Nothing.

"Dead," I mutter, sliding it back into my pocket. "My last connection to civilization. Gone."

"There's a satellite phone for emergencies." He doesn't even look up. "Radio too. Storms make it unreliable."

"Thanks, doomsday prepper." I sigh. "Wasn't looking to call 911. Just... Instagram. Or maybe my assistant. She'll think I've joined a cult."

"They'll manage."

His voice is so even, so maddeningly calm. Like he doesn't get rattled. Like he's never once thrown his phone at a wall or ugly-cried over a dead charger.

"True." I wander to the window, watching rain cascade down the glass. "Still weird to be completely cut off."

We settle into our silences like two people learning to breathe the same air.

He scribbles in a weather log or field journal or whatever rugged survivalists write in, posture relaxed, boots planted wide, concentration etched into every hard line of his face. I scroll through old photos, pretending to work, pretending I'm not hyperaware of every shift of his body, every creak of the chair beneath his weight.

The fire crackles low.

The storm howls against the eaves.

And the cabin... it changes.

Not romantic. No.

But warm.

Settled.

Like this place—this strange, isolated world we've stumbled into—has its own gravity.

God help me, I'm starting to like the quiet.

As dusk crawls across the cabin and settles in like a blanket, my stomach betrays me loudly. The growl ricochets off the log walls, embarrassing and impossible to ignore. I glance toward the kitchenette. Then at Caleb.

He hasn't moved from his desk. Still scribbling away like he's single-handedly solving climate change, war, and the meaning of life with nothing but a dull pencil and sheer willpower. That brow is furrowed in concentration, lips pressed into a thin line, and those maddening hands—those hands—grip the pen with quiet command.

I think about asking if he's hungry. Maybe offer to cook

something. Though my idea of cooking mostly involves microwave buttons and an emotional commitment to crackers, cheese, and shame. But before I can embarrass myself further, he shifts.

Chair scrapes back. He stands.

And stretches.

Arms up. Shirt rides up. Muscles ripple under flannel, the hem lifting just enough to flash skin—tan, tight, sinfully cut. My brain short-circuits. All thoughts deleted. Replaced by a mental slideshow titled Things I Could Do to That Torso.

"Hungry?" he asks, like he didn't just unleash an erotic apocalypse on my nervous system.

"Starving." My answer's too quick, too high, like I'm auditioning for a game show instead of trying not to combust.

He moves to the fridge with that same quiet efficiency that's starting to undo me, one steady footfall at a time. Pulls out a handful of vegetables, a container of cooked rice, a carton of eggs. His movements are exact, practiced. There's a plan forming in his head, and I watch it play out in real time.

He grabs a chef's knife and starts chopping like it's second nature. Confident. Fluid. Precise. I can't help but wonder what else those hands have learned to master.

"Need an assistant chef?" I offer, inching closer, helpless against the magnetic pull of his space.

"No."

One word. No glance. Just the firm brush-off of a man who knows how to work alone.

Onions hit the hot pan, followed by garlic, oil, and something spicy that bites at the back of my throat and settles lower —warm and wicked. The scent wraps around me like temptation in steam form.

"Almost done," he adds, tossing chopped peppers like he's conducting an orchestra made of heat and hunger.

Of course, he's almost done. Of course, he cooks like this. Methodical. Silent. Focused. Like he's locked in a staring contest with the skillet and refuses to blink until he's won.

I lean back against the counter, useless and captivated, trying to look anywhere but at his forearms flexing with each flick of the wrist.

But I fail. Spectacularly.

And when he reaches for the soy sauce, tilts the pan, and gives it a controlled shake that sends the scent of toasted sesame and pure masculine competence into the air—I swear to God, I nearly moan.

Someone save me. Or don't. Honestly, I'm fine dying like this.

When he sets the plate in front of me a few minutes later, I nearly weep. It's just vegetables and rice, but it smells like five-star comfort food. Like warmth and muscle memory and hands that build and nourish in equal measure. The scent alone could melt resolve.

"This looks amazing," I breathe, already half-moaning as I inhale the steam curling off the plate. "I wasn't expecting gourmet mountain cuisine."

"It's just food." His voice is low, unbothered. But there's a flicker—barely there—in the corners of his mouth. Pride, betrayed for just a second.

I take the first bite, and my brain short-circuits. Garlic and ginger sing at the edges. Something smoky curls at the back of my tongue. A hit of spice lingers low, like a secret. My eyes flutter closed, pleasure sinking deep.

"This is..." I shake my head, reverent. "Culinary foreplay. Honestly. Where'd you learn to cook like this?"

He pauses, just long enough to register. "My crew. Hotshots. We rotated cooking duties at base camp."

Hotshots.

The word lands like a match tossed on dry brush. Firefighters. Elite ones. Suddenly the quiet control, the lethal grace, the intensity that clings to him like smoke—they all make sense.

I don't push. Not yet.

"That explains the practical skills," I say lightly, chasing the thought of him in fire gear, soot-streaked and adrenaline-laced, hauling people from the flames.

He just nods. Eyes down. Focused on his food like it's safer than me.

Then I blow it.

"I saw a newspaper article earlier." The words tumble out like spilled wine—too fast, impossible to clean up. "About your crew. Mountain fire. You saved—"

"You went through my things?"

The shift is instant. Not dramatic. Not loud. Just—still. The kind of still that makes your skin tighten, because something primal has entered the room. He doesn't look at me. Doesn't move. Just freezes, like a blade held breath-close.

"No—well, not exactly," I fumble, heart thudding. "The chest under your desk was open. The clipping was right there. I didn't dig. I was just curious…"

His eyes finally lift. Green and unreadable. "Curiosity doesn't justify invading my privacy."

The air goes razor thin. His voice isn't loud, but it hums with something restrained and dangerous. Not rage. Worse. Disappointment.

Silence stretches. Long enough for my breath to feel loud in my own ears. My skin prickles.

"You're right." My voice is soft. Steady. "I'm sorry." I set my fork down, the clink of metal on ceramic sharper than it should be. "I shouldn't have looked. Not without permission."

And I mean it. Every word. But I don't look away. Not this time.

Because beneath the apology, something else pulses—connection. Delicate. Frayed at the edges. And still holding.

He studies me for a long moment, jaw tight, lips parted just slightly like the words are there, lodged somewhere between memory and restraint. Muscles tick in his cheek. He looks like a man walking barefoot across broken glass—aware of every sharp edge, every misstep waiting to cut.

Then, finally, a breath. A soft exhale that sounds like surrender.

"It was the Carson Ridge Fire. 2018." His voice is rough, stripped bare. "We got twelve hikers out before the fire jumped the containment line."

I watch him in profile, the cut of his jaw in the low cabin light, the flicker of something old and raw in his eyes.

"Twelve hikers rescued. Three firefighters injured. One fatality." My voice is quiet, careful. But it still lands like a match in dry brush.

His jaw flexes, and for a second, I want to bite my tongue. Take it back. Let him keep the silence he's made into armor.

"You were the one who went back in, weren't you?"

He doesn't answer at first. Just lets the moment stretch until I feel it hum beneath my skin. Then he nods once. Slow. Heavy.

I should stop. I know I should stop. Let him have this boundary. Let him change the subject.

But I don't. Because he didn't shut me out. Because the ache behind his eyes is too human to ignore.

"What happened?"

He turns his head and looks at me. Really looks. And what I see in his eyes isn't just memory—it's flame. Pain. Guilt. Fierce, relentless love. All braided together in a knot he doesn't know how to untangle.

"We'd already pulled everyone out," he says. Each word is deliberate, like it costs him something. "Or thought we had. Then we got a call—a kid, separated from his family. Smoke thick as concrete. Fire jumping ridges like it was chasing ghosts."

"You went in."

He shrugs, like it was nothing. Like racing into hell was just another Tuesday. "Didn't think. Just moved."

But I see the way his hand curls into a fist against his thigh. The way his breath stutters—so slight, so controlled.

My throat closes. "And your teammate?"

A pause. And then he says it, flat and brutal.

"Didn't make it." He looks away, a muscle ticking in his jaw.

The room is so quiet, even the fire seems to hold its breath.

He doesn't explain. Doesn't elaborate. Just stares at some invisible point on the floorboards like if he focuses hard enough, he can hold the memory still. Or maybe bury it.

I want to reach for him. To offer touch. Warmth. Something.

But I don't.

Because I don't think he's ever said those words out loud, and in this moment, holding space for them feels more sacred than any comfort I could give.

I don't reach for him. He wouldn't want that. But I see him. The grief he carries like it's stitched into his skin. The way he's built his whole life around silence, solitude, and surviving the wreckage.

"You saved that kid," I whisper.

"I left someone behind," he snaps, then exhales like the words cost him something. "I don't need a medal for doing my job. Definitely *not* for getting a teammate get killed."

I shake my head. "No medal. Just... someone who sees you."

He blinks at me. Like he doesn't know what to do with that.

With me.

The concession, small as it is, feels significant. I nod, accepting the information without pushing for more.

"Your turn." He takes a bite of food, eyes still on me. "Why chase eagles in storm season?"

"My father was a wildlife photographer. The golden eagle was his white whale—he spent twenty years trying to capture the perfect shot." I smile at the memory. "He died two years ago, his collection incomplete."

"So you're finishing it for him."

"Trying to. I've got shots of forty-seven of the forty-eight species he documented. The eagle is the last one."

"Why now? Storm season isn't ideal for photography."

"Eagles nest in spring. This was my window." I shrug, not mentioning the anniversary of Dad's death approaching, the deadline I've set for myself to complete what he couldn't.

Caleb nods, something like understanding crossing his features. We finish eating in companionable silence, the earlier tension eased by this exchange of personal truths, however small.

Our brief exchange, rather than feeling like a normal conversation, feels as if I've fought a battle, and I don't know if I've lost or won.

It's hard to concentrate when I can feel him across the table—every shift of muscle, every breath. There's a low, steady tension under his calm. A restraint I'm starting to suspect doesn't stop at the surface.

And damn it, I want to find out just how far it goes.

We finish eating in silence, but it's not awkward anymore. It's thick. Taut. Like the whole cabin is holding its breath with us, waiting for the spark to hit the wire.

I move to gather the plates, but he pushes his chair back at the same time. "I've got it."

"No way. You cooked. I'll clean." I bump him aside with my hip, an accidental move that feels anything but accidental. His hand comes to my lower back—light, fleeting, maddeningly gentle. But that touch? It lands like a strike of lightning. Just a brush of rough warmth and I forget how to function.

But it's enough. The contact disappears, but the heat stays.

Enough to make me hyperaware of the space between us. Of how warm he is. Of the subtle scent that clings to him—pine and smoke and something that's just him.

We fall into rhythm at the sink, passing plates and utensils, our fingers brushing again and again. Each accidental contact ratchets the tension higher. Every touch is like a spark we both pretend not to notice.

But we notice.

He hands me a pot. His fingers close around mine—just for a heartbeat too long. My breath stumbles. My gaze snaps to his. His eyes drop to my mouth, linger for half a second, and lift again. His jaw tightens like he's biting back a decision he doesn't trust himself to make.

Say something. Do something. Just breathe.

I want to ask what he's thinking. I want to throw the dish towel and kiss him senseless. I do neither.

Instead, I dry the damn pot and pretend my pulse isn't trying to escape through my throat and I'm not seconds from combusting.

We finish the dishes in silence after that. But it's a different kind of quiet. Not empty. Full.

Full of the truth he let slip. Full of all the things we're not saying. Full of heat and guilt and whatever this thing is sparking between us.

By the time we finish, I'm flushed and breathless, like we

ran a marathon instead of doing dishes. He moves away first, breaking the moment like it cost him something. Maybe it did.

Night falls early in the mountains, darkness pressing against the windows. Rain continues its steady assault, the earlier downpour settling into a consistent patter that promises to continue through the night.

When he moves away to stoke the fire again, I let myself look. Really look. At the man who walks through fire and still carries the burn. At the strength, the solitude, and the surprising softness under all that gruff.

I pretend not to watch the flex of his back as he adds logs to the stove. The room fills with warmth, but I'm already burning.

The silence stretches again, deeper now, layered with everything we didn't say and all the things I'm suddenly aching to.

The domestic scene feels strangely intimate—the two of us enclosed in this small space, surrounded by the vastness of wilderness.

"I'll take the floor tonight." He breaks the silence, nodding toward the back room. "You keep the bed."

And just like that, the spell shatters.

"That's ridiculous. This is your home. I should take the floor."

"You're injured." He gestures to my knee, the bandage visible through the tear in my pants.

"It's just a scrape. Besides, the floor's hard. Cold."

"All the more reason you shouldn't sleep on it." The line is delivered with such quiet finality, it's not worth arguing.

Still, I try.

"At least alternate nights." I cross my arms, matching his stubborn stance.

"No."

"Why not?"

"Because I'm not taking a bed while my guest sleeps on the floor." The statement has the weight of an immovable principle behind it. "And because I said so."

God, he's infuriating. Infuriating and principled and hot as sin. And, since my fantasies have hijacked my mind, I love the way he said that. *Because I said so.* Damn, light a match and let me burn.

"Fine." I throw up my hands. "But I'm not happy about it."

"Noted." His lips twitch. The ghost of a smile, and it hits harder than a full grin from anyone else.

He unrolls a sleeping bag by the woodstove like it's the most natural thing in the world—like giving up his bed is no big deal.

But it is.

It's a massive deal, and I feel that deal in every beat of my suddenly traitorous heart.

"Caleb, seriously—"

"It's decided." He cuts me off with a finality that brooks no argument. "Bathroom's yours if you want it."

I retreat to prepare for bed, borrowing a t-shirt he's grudgingly offered as sleepwear. When I return to the main room, he's dimmed the lights, leaving only the glow from the woodstove to illuminate the space.

"Goodnight, then." I hover awkwardly, still uncomfortable with the arrangement.

"Night." He's already in the sleeping bag, hands behind his head, staring at the ceiling.

In the back room, I crawl into his bed and pull the covers up, his scent wrapping around me. Clean laundry, pine, woodsmoke... and something darker. Something dangerous.

Despite the cot's narrowness, it's reasonably comfortable, certainly better than the floor. Still, guilt needles me at the thought of Caleb's tall frame confined to a sleeping bag while I take his bed.

I lie there for hours, listening to the rain, the fire, and the slow, steady rhythm of his breathing.

And wondering why the most infuriating man I've ever met is also the one I most want to touch.

Angel's Peak

Chapter 5

Sunlight pierces the small window, falling across my face. Into my eyes. No rest for the weary, not that I've been excessively active. For a moment, I lie still, orienting myself once again to this unfamiliar space. The ranger station. Angel's Peak.

Caleb.

The events of yesterday filter through my consciousness—the tree fall, the rain, the awkward dinner that somehow bridged a fraction of the distance between us. I stretch, wincing at the stiffness in my muscles, before padding to the door and peering into the main room.

Caleb stands at the kitchenette with his back to me, the sleeping bag already rolled and stowed. His hair is damp from a shower, the dark strands curling slightly at his nape. Something about this unguarded moment makes my chest tighten inexplicably.

"Morning." My voice sounds too loud in the quiet cabin.

He turns, coffee mug in hand. "Storm's passed. Temporarily."

I move to the window, greedy for the view after being

confined by yesterday's rain. Sunlight bathes the mountainside, transforming raindrops into diamonds on pine needles and turning puddles into mirrors reflecting the impossibly blue sky. The forest looks newborn, vibrant greens intensified by their recent washing.

"Beautiful." The word escapes on a breath, more to myself than to Caleb.

"Best time in the mountains. Right after a storm." He joins me at the window, maintaining a careful distance. "Everything washed clean."

I glance at him, surprised by the almost poetic observation from this taciturn man. "Exactly."

He clears his throat, retreating from this brief moment of shared appreciation. "Need to check the wildlife shelters. Make sure they weathered the storm."

"Wildlife shelters?"

"Rehabilitation enclosures. For injured animals." He hesitates, then adds, "You can come. If you want."

The invitation catches me off guard. "I'd like that."

"We leave in twenty minutes."

While he prepares supplies, I rush through getting ready, excitement building at the prospect of finally getting outside. My clothes have dried overnight, hanging near the woodstove. My boots, still damp but wearable, wait by the door.

I retrieve my backup camera from my bag—a smaller model than my professional one, but it survived in its waterproof case. Better than nothing if we encounter anything worth capturing.

Caleb hands me a protein bar and a travel mug of coffee like we're a married couple heading out for a hike instead of two strangers barely on speaking terms. "Breakfast on the move."

Be still, my ovaries.

His fingers brush mine, and it takes every ounce of self-control not to suck in a breath like some virginal schoolgirl. Not that there's anything virginal about the thoughts currently occupying 98% of my brain.

The morning air is crisp enough to bite, rich with the scent of pine needles crushed underfoot, damp earth, and moss still soaked from last night's storm. But under all that—threaded through like some sinful secret—is him. That maddening mix of sweat, cedar, and clean skin, like he just stepped out of a cold shower and straight into my last coherent thought.

It's infuriating, really. He lives like a damn hermit, chops wood with a glare, probably thinks body wash is a luxury for the weak—and still manages to smell like every forbidden craving I've ever had.

Water drips from the branches overhead, a slow patter of sound that blends with the crunch of our boots on the trail. One rogue drop slips down the collar of my jacket, trailing along my spine like a cold finger. I shiver and pull the zipper higher, though it does nothing to shield me from the other kind of chill creeping through me—the kind born of watching him move.

Caleb walks ahead, every step a lesson in wilderness poetry. Graceful. Grounded. Like the forest shifts around him instead of the other way around. Muscles flex beneath his cargo pants, each stride tugging my gaze lower no matter how many times I remind myself to be an adult. A professional. Not some drooling cavewoman with a tree fetish.

But God, that ass. Carved by divine spite and covered in tactical fabric that should be illegal. Every flex, every roll of muscle makes my thighs clench in protest, like they're auditioning for a role I didn't sign them up for.

Focus, I command myself. Eyes up. Mind out of the gutter.

But the gutter is warm, and it smells like him.

My knee throbs, still tender from twisting it yesterday, but I push through. Not because I'm brave. Hell no. Because I refuse to be the whining city girl who can't keep up with the mountain god who probably bench-presses grizzlies for fun and whose voice I just mentally used in a very vivid tree-bondage fantasy.

"How far are these shelters?" I ask, more to break the fever dream than for actual information. My voice comes out too breathy, too high. Like I've been running. Or fantasizing about him dragging me off-trail and saying get on your knees and beg me.

He glances back. Eyes flick from my face to my feet, lingering long enough to catch the flush creeping up my throat. And then higher. Straight into my eyes.

There's a flicker there—something unreadable. Knowing. Disapproving. Maybe amused.

"Half a mile further."

That's it. No reaction. No smirk. Just that sharp, steady gaze like he's already guessed exactly what I've been thinking and filed it under unacceptable behavior from forest guests.

I clear my throat, look away, and try to think about anything other than bark texture, rope tension, or the way his voice would sound murmuring good girl against my neck.

God help me. This hike is going to kill me. And if it doesn't, the tension will.

I school my features into something that—if you squint—might pass for composed, even though my brain is still in full-blown erotica narrator mode. Somewhere between nature documentary and filthy rope-play fantasy, I'm mentally scripting a scene where that calloused hand wraps around my throat while he pins me to a tree and makes me beg.

"Need to rest?" he asks, his tone maddeningly neutral.

Bastard.

"No." I straighten like pride alone can brace my knee, even as pain pulses down my leg like a warning flare. "I'm fine."

One eyebrow lifts, a flick of dry skepticism that says *Sure you are*, but he doesn't argue.

Because he's decent.

Respectful.

And clearly unaware that I've mentally ridden him in at least six positions since breakfast—including one that involved rope, a rock wall, and me saying thank you with tears in my eyes.

And I haven't even finished my protein bar.

The trail breaks open into a sun-drenched clearing, all filtered gold light and pine shadows, where several structures sit spaced like tiny cabins. Each one's enclosed in wire mesh and roofed with weatherproof paneling. Wildlife shelters. Or maybe thirst traps, since Caleb is already stalking toward the first one with quiet, devastating purpose.

I hang back under the guise of giving him room, but really? I need a minute. Or twelve. To reset. Breathe. Maybe dunk my head in a creek.

Because watching him move is a violation of every decency law I pretend to follow. The flannel strains across his shoulders as he crouches beside the first feeding station, his spine curving with perfect, dangerous intent. His jeans—soaked in places from trail spray—cling to every muscle they have no business showcasing. And when he bends low enough for the fabric to tighten across his thighs?

I swear my uterus makes a sound.

How does he not know what he looks like?

What that body is doing to me?

What it's capable of doing?

I sip lukewarm coffee, pretending to focus on the enclosures, while my mind invents ways to trap us both in a conveniently collapsing shelter where I'm forced to wrap my legs around his waist for "stability."

Or mouth-to-mouth.

Or mutual survival-induced orgasms.

I'm flexible.

"What kind of animals do you rehabilitate here?" My voice barely works, breathy and uneven. I need the distraction. Anything to stop picturing him naked in that same position, jaw tight, hands busy, fixing something I very much broke on purpose.

"Depends." He checks a metal tray filled with seed, his broad back to me. "Mostly injured birds. Small mammals. Orphans. Things that wouldn't make it on their own."

A deep breath rattles through my lungs. Focus on the animals. Not the man. The innocent creatures. The wholesome mission. Not his arms or the way his voice does that thing where it drops half an octave and makes me want to cry.

"You do all the care yourself?"

He moves to the next structure, doesn't look back.

"Part of the job."

Of course it is. Of course, he's not just sexy. He's an off-grid, animal-rescuing, gear-hauling, wilderness-cooking, emotionally repressed Greek tragedy in plaid. I bet he bathes baby deer with biodegradable soap and reads bedtime stories to injured raccoons.

If he tells me he once bottle-fed an orphaned possum while simultaneously performing CPR on a kestrel, I'll strip right here in the pine needles.

I follow him through the clearing, taking photos of the shelters with unsteady hands. Most are empty, their trays full, latches secured. But one enclosure isn't vacant. Inside, perched on a smooth branch, a red-tailed hawk stares back at me— majestic, proud, still.

"She's beautiful," I whisper, lifting my camera to frame the bird's profile.

Caleb crouches beside the mesh. "Wing fracture," he murmurs, voice gentling in a way that gut-punches something tender inside me. "She's healing well. Maybe another week, then release."

That softness. That reverence. It wraps around my ribs and tightens, aching in a place I didn't know could ache for anything but lust.

I don't know whether I want to kiss him or sob.

Maybe both.

He moves to the final shelter, and I follow, watching the slight crease between his brows deepen as he inspects a warped latch. Focused. Quiet. Diligent.

He works like I imagine he fucks—steady hands, full attention, unhurried confidence. Not just doing the job.

Mastering it.

And suddenly, the phrase *wildlife rehabilitation* takes on an entirely different meaning.

Mmmmm...those hands.

I trail behind him like a lovesick idiot with a camera, pretending I'm here for the wildlife and not the walking wilderness fantasy currently five steps ahead of me. I capture everything—the way sunlight slants through the trees like golden blades, how the wire mesh catches the light in sharp angles, how leaves rustle like secrets overhead. But it's Caleb who keeps ending up in the center of every frame.

Always Caleb.

Bent forward, crouched low, stretching tall. Each movement is an accidental masterpiece I want to study with my mouth.

When he finishes checking the last enclosure, he straightens slowly. There's a moment—a pause so still it hums —where he scans the clearing like he's reading it. Not with logic, but instinct. That quiet, animal sense that says he doesn't just exist here—he belongs here. Shadow and sunlight stripe his face like war paint, and something inside me goes molten.

He hesitates. I see it in the subtle tick of his jaw, the flick of his gaze toward me. Then away. Like he's debating something.

Please let it be whether or not to kiss me.

Or ruin me.

Or both.

Anything that ends with that mouth on mine, on skin, on the soft places I pretend aren't already aching for him.

I keep my expression casual, like my brain isn't melting into erotica about tree bark and flannel. But if he could read my thoughts? He'd never look at another bird feeder the same way again.

"There's another spot," he says finally, voice low. "If you're interested."

I nod, way too fast. "Always."

"Fox den. Quarter mile east. Cubs were born last month."

My heart does a stupid, eager flutter. And... yeah. So does everything else.

"Lead the way."

Angel's Peak

CHAPTER 6

The trail narrows immediately, crowded by dense underbrush and wet ferns, forcing us into single file. Caleb steps ahead, and I try—really try—not to stare at the hypnotic flex of his back under that damn flannel or the way his jeans hug his thighs with the kind of reverence I fully understand.

He walks like a man who doesn't waste movement. Like he's carved from the same granite that anchors this forest.

Each step is exact.

Controlled.

Dangerous in a way that has nothing to do with predators and everything to do with what it would feel like to be trapped beneath him, pinned between that body and the earth, learning the weight of restraint undone.

And here I am.

Aroused.

By forestry.

Again.

Great.

The storm-wet trail tries to trip me with every step—mud

grabbing at my boots, ferns dragging across my thighs. But I keep up. Not just because I want to. Because I need to. Caleb doesn't speak, but every shift of his shoulders, every precise placement of his feet, feels like a command.

And I follow.

Because I'd follow that man into a wildfire with nothing but a camera and a bad idea.

He stops so suddenly that I nearly crash into him.

One hand lifts—a silent signal.

I freeze.

His body turns, just enough for his breath to brush my cheek, warm and woodsmoke-scented. "Fox." The word grazes my ear like a sin I want to commit twice.

That one syllable shouldn't make my thighs clench. It shouldn't short-circuit my entire pelvic floor. But it does.

Because it's him.

Because he says it like it matters. Like everything does. Every word. Every look. Every brush of skin that hasn't happened yet but might.

And I want it to.

God, I want it to.

His gaze flicks toward the brush ahead, and I follow it, willing my heartbeat to slow down, willing my hormones to take a goddamn seat.

There are fox cubs ahead.

Baby animals.

Innocent, fragile nature.

Please, brain. For once. Don't turn this into foreplay.

Too late.

Here we are.

I follow his gaze toward a fallen log. At first, I see nothing. Then—a flicker of russet against bark, so perfectly camouflaged it takes a trained eye to spot.

He has a trained eye. And I have dirty thoughts. It's a partnership.

My camera comes up automatically, my fingers instinctively adjusting the settings. The lens locks onto a sleek copper form—mother fox, ears swiveling, alert but calm. Then three cubs spill out behind her like a ball of ginger chaos, tumbling over each other in the morning sun.

The shutter is nearly silent. But Caleb winces.

"Too loud."

"They can't hear it from this distance," I murmur, not taking my eye from the viewfinder. "Silent shutter. I'm not a total amateur."

His eyes narrow, skepticism flashing, but when the foxes don't flinch, he relaxes again. Satisfied.

We fall into silence. Twenty whole minutes pass in reverent quiet—me documenting, him just... watching. And not in that casual 'look at the cute animals' way either. No, he watches like he's memorizing them. Like every detail matters. And damn it if that kind of quiet intensity doesn't do something to me.

"The smallest one is struggling." His voice is barely audible. "See how the others push him away from food?"

I shift the focus to the runt. He's right—the little one keeps getting shouldered aside by its siblings. My heart tugs. Of course, he noticed. Mr. Taciturn Woodsman with the unexpected emotional radar.

"Nature can be cruel."

"Not always." He points again, this time to the mother repositioning herself to allow the smallest cub access to her belly. "They adapt. Find solutions."

His tone's different now. Softer. Invested. And oh great, now my uterus is writing sonnets about him.

I lower my camera, turning to study him instead. The way the sunlight filters through the trees and lights up the side of his face. The faint crow's feet at the corners of his eyes. The curve of his mouth—not smiling, not frowning, just quiet... content.

"You know a lot about them."

"Been monitoring this family three seasons." There's unmistakable pride in his voice, and something warmer beneath it. "Mother was injured last winter. Treated her here. Released her in February."

"Just in time to have her cubs."

He nods. And then—there it is. The faintest twitch at the corner of his mouth. A ghost of a smile. Not sarcastic. Not guarded. Real. Soft. Like it snuck past his defenses before he could stop it.

"Success story," he says, eyes fixed on the den like it means more than he'll ever admit.

I should be taking pictures. That's why I'm here. Capture the wildlife, document the moment, do my job. And I do— two quick shots of the foxes as they tumble near the log, a blur of russet and tiny paws. But my lens drifts.

Up.

To him.

To the way he's kneeling, one forearm resting on his bent knee, the soft curve of that almost-smile still haunting his mouth. The peace on his face. The quiet reverence in the way he watches them—like he knows what it took for this moment to exist.

That's the shot. Right there. That's the story.

The man who saved a mother fox, alone in the woods, and watched her bring new life into the world like it's no big deal. Like it's just part of the job.

He doesn't even notice me watching him.

And I don't stop looking. Don't stop thinking about what it would be like if he ever turned that same focus—calm, consuming, tenderness—on me.

Spoiler alert: it ends with me against a tree, my clothes somewhere in the underbrush, and a very smug fox cub as witness.

We stay until the mother slips back beneath the log, her cubs following in tumbling sequence. A last flicker of russet vanishes into the den, and the clearing empties, like a curtain falling on a performance.

Then silence. Stillness. The clearing empties out like the end of a show, and all that's left is the sound of wind through the pines and the thrum in my chest I can't seem to shut off.

As we turn away, Caleb surprises me. "Could check on them again tomorrow. If the weather holds." Low. Casual. But there's a hesitation in it—a flicker of something cracking through that controlled wilderness he wears like armor.

An invitation.

And not just to see the foxes.

A flicker of something cracking through all that controlled wilderness he wears like armor.

"I'd like that."

We walk again, but the air's changed. Less distance. Less silence. Something's shifted between us, and I feel it with every step.

Caleb leads us along a different path, pointing out flora and rock formations I never would've noticed—if I weren't already laser-focused on every damn thing he says. His voice, low and gravel-edged, rolls over me like warm smoke. He talks about watershed erosion and soil pH and lichen colonies, but all I hear is bedroom voice.

I mean, come on.

He says "phosphorus retention" like it's foreplay. Describes the root system of a ponderosa pine like it's the opening line to a smutty novella. I'm not okay.

I don't even know what watershed density is, but I'd beg him to explain it again, slower, while unbuttoning his shirt.

I learn more about Angel's Peak in an hour than any guidebook could've told me. I also learn that I want this man —this infuriating, enigmatic, maddeningly restrained man— to do unspeakable things to me against a moss-covered boulder.

Because that voice—warm smoke and midnight woodfire —makes my skin feel tight. Makes me think about beds made of pine needles and what it would feel like to have that voice right at my ear while those hands made me forget my name.

"The mountain creates its own weather system," he says, pausing to gesture toward the peaks in the distance. "Cold air off the northern ridge meets the valley's warm updrafts. Triggers instability."

He stops to lift a fallen branch off the trail, forearms flexing beneath rolled sleeves. The kind of strength that doesn't brag. Doesn't pose. Just is.

I swear the air gets warmer. Or maybe that's just me, burning from the inside out while pretending to care about lichen colonies.

I follow him.

God help me, I'd follow him anywhere.

The air shifts—brighter one moment, darker the next. Clouds bloom like bruises above the ridgeline. The wind carries a bite now, teasing through the trees, stirring the hem of my damp shirt.

"More rain coming?" I glance up, tracking the roiling sky.

"Probably." He frowns. "Sooner than forecast."

Spoiler alert: *very soon.*

The first raindrop lands with an icy kiss on my collarbone. Then another. Then—

Downpour.

We don't speak, just break into a run, boots slapping mud. The wind howls as if it's got something to prove, rain pelting down in a sudden onslaught that soaks us in seconds. My clothes cling like a second skin, plastered to every inch of me, cold enough to raise goosebumps—and heat enough to burn right through them.

"This way." Caleb grabs my elbow. Just his hand—rough, warm, anchoring.

He veers off the trail toward a low silhouette tucked against the ridge. A structure. I hadn't even noticed it.

We reach the door in a sprint, half-blind from the rain. Caleb throws it open, practically shoves me inside before following, slamming it shut behind us.

The slam echoes.

Silence follows.

The shelter is barely bigger than a closet. Wooden walls, narrow bench, weather station gear in one corner, and a single battery-powered lantern on the shelf. No electricity. No distractions.

Just us. A one-room cabin, and one bed.

Just kill me now.

Angel's Peak

Chapter 7

Water streams off me—hair plastered to my scalp, jacket clinging like a second skin. I'm soaked to the bone, shivering, half-mad with cold and something far more dangerous.

But he's worse.

Caleb stands in the middle of the cabin like some feral deity summoned by thunder, his shirt molded to his chest like wet paint. Every ridge, every defined edge of muscle etched in high-def torment. Pecs. Abs. Veins that snake down thick forearms made for lifting, gripping, holding someone in place while they come undone.

Jesus.

He looks like wrath sculpted in flesh. Like sin carved from stone and left to weather in the wild.

And I want to climb him. Wrap myself around him like ivy and beg to be torn apart.

A violent shiver racks me. Not just from the cold this time.

He notices. Of course he fucking does.

Caleb shrugs off his soaked jacket, muscles rippling like a

warning. Then grabs a blanket from the shelf and tosses it toward me without a word.

"You're soaked."

No shit, Ranger Rude and Repressed. But sure—let's pretend like this is about weather.

I catch the blanket, fingers trembling, and wrap it around my body like armor. As if wool can protect me from the hunger burning low and deep. As if I'm not seconds from combusting.

Then his hands go to the hem of his shirt.

Oh God.

He peels it off in one smooth pull—water sluicing down his torso, catching on the curve of his chest, the dip of his stomach, the line of a scar slicing across his side like a memory of fire.

And I break.

My mouth actually drops open. Like a damn cartoon character. Like I've never seen a shirtless man before in my life.

Holy hell.

He's not just ripped—he's ruinous. Like a Roman statue got tired of being admired and decided to learn how to throw a woman over his shoulder and wreck her worldview instead.

My hands twitch with the need to touch. To trace the cut of his hips. To map every scar with my tongue and learn the story of his body through taste and sweat and surrender. I want to fall to my knees in front of him and offer everything— breath, restraint, control—and watch his face as I do it.

Lightning flares outside, blinding for a split second. His silhouette glows sharp and wild—jaw clenched, hair damp and curling at the nape, eyes locked on mine like he hears every single thought I shouldn't be thinking.

Thunder answers—low, rolling, obscene.

The room smells like smoke, pine, ozone, and him. The air is thick with it. With us.

I can't look away.

Don't want to.

Because if he touches me now—if he takes even one step forward—I'll burn alive.

And I'll beg for it.

His gaze lifts to mine, slow and deliberate, like he's peeling back layers I didn't know I had. And just like that, the air in the shelter shifts—thick with heat, with want, with something neither of us is saying.

"You're staring." His voice is low. Rough. The kind of sound that curls around your spine and whispers don't stop.

"You're not exactly easy to look away from."

The words leave my mouth before I can catch them. Honest. Raw. Soaked-through-and-horny truth with no filter and even less shame.

He doesn't smile. Doesn't flirt. Just watches me.

And it does feel like watching—like I'm under a lens, like he's studying every flicker of my breath, every tremble I try to hide. His eyes stay locked on mine, unreadable and steady, until they flick—just once—down to my mouth.

Oh.

Oh, hell.

I feel it. A jolt, pure and physical, snapping through me like lightning striking too close to home. The kind of tension that hums beneath the skin. Dangerous. Addictive.

One more look. One more breath.

And I'm going to do something reckless.

Something irrevocable.

And he's either going to stop me.

Or help me come apart in his hands.

Honestly, either would be fine.

Thunder cracks directly overhead—loud enough to rattle the walls, shake the floor, send my pulse into overdrive. I flinch. More from the break in the moment than the sound itself. My body moves before I think—closer to him. Seeking warmth. Grounding. Shelter in the form of his impossible body and maddening restraint.

He doesn't step back. Doesn't reach for me either. Just stands there, rain-slick and bare-chested, eyes burning with something I can't name, chest rising in slow, even rhythm.

Like he's unaffected.

Like he didn't just watch me fall halfway in lust with him in real time.

The tension lingers. Still thick. Still electric. But the spell has cracked around the edges.

The rain pours harder. The sky growls above us.

And I grab for the nearest excuse. Anything to get my hands to stop shaking and my brain to start pretending this isn't what it is.

"Storms scared me when I was a kid," I blurt. Too fast. Too bright. My voice is a brittle thing between us. "My dad would make me count the seconds between lightning and thunder. Said if I understood it, I wouldn't be afraid."

I look anywhere but at him. At the wall. The blanket. My own damn hands.

Because I was this close to kissing him.

Caleb doesn't speak right away. Just watches me, something softer flickering behind that guarded expression.

"Smart man."

"He was." The answer slips out more raw than I expect. My throat tightens. Emotion sneaks up on me like the cold had earlier—sudden, uninvited, impossible to ignore. I look away, pretending to study the rivulets of water racing down the windowpane. "That's why this project matters. It's not just about the photographs."

When I glance back at him, his gaze is steady. Grounding. Not just interested—listening.

"What is it about?"

"Finishing what he started." I swallow hard. "He spent thirty years documenting predatory birds—one perfect photo of each species found in North America. The golden eagle was the one that got away. His white whale."

"You mentioned that." A ghost of a smile pulls at the corner of Caleb's mouth. "You promised to get it for him."

"I did." The words come out quiet. "He passed two years ago. And I told myself I'd finish the collection. Complete his work. Even if I had to chase a storm across a mountain to do it."

The rain drums harder, wind whistling through the gaps in the shelter's seams, but in here it's oddly still. Not warm— but no longer cold either.

"You get it yet?" Caleb asks.

"Not yet," I murmur. "But I'm close. I can feel it."

He nods, gaze distant for a beat. Then: "He'd be proud."

I blink.

Simple words. But they hit harder than anything I expected.

"Thanks," I whisper, throat tightening again—but not from sadness this time. "That means more than you know."

We fall into silence again, but it's different now. No longer charged with heat or awkwardness, but something quieter. He slides down to sit on the bench, resting his elbows on his knees, and I take the other end, careful to leave space between us this time.

He passes me the lantern, and for a moment our fingers brush—cool skin to warm, steady hands to jittery ones.

But this time, I don't mistake the contact for an invitation.

This time, I just breathe in the quiet. And let it settle.

"How did your father die?" he asks.

"Heart attack. He was on a shoot in Wyoming. By the time I got there..." I swallow hard. "Photography was our connection. After my parents divorced, weekends with Dad meant hiking with cameras, chasing wildlife."

"That's why you pushed on despite the storm."

"Yeah." I smile ruefully. "Dad always said the best shots come when other photographers have packed up and gone home."

Another shiver runs through me, more pronounced this time. Without comment, Caleb shifts closer, hesitantly placing his arm around my shoulders. The gesture is awkward, tentative, as though he's forgotten how human contact works. But his body radiates heat, and I find myself leaning into his warmth.

"Your turn." I glance up at him, suddenly aware of our proximity, the weight of his arm, the subtle scent of pine and rain that clings to him. "Why did you leave firefighting?"

His body tenses, but he doesn't withdraw. "Long story."

"We've got time." I gesture to the storm outside. "Unless you have somewhere pressing to be."

A ghost of a smile touches his lips, there and gone. He's silent for so long, I think he won't answer. When he finally speaks, his voice is low, as if sharing a confidence he's held close for years.

"Sometimes you can do everything right and still lose."

The weight of unsaid words hangs between us. I wait, sensing there's more.

"I quit after Carson Ridge." His voice is low, flat—but his jaw flexes like the memory still draws blood.

I go still. Understanding slams into me like a falling tree. "Caleb..."

"Like I said. Long story."

His gaze cuts away, evasive. But his arm doesn't move.

Doesn't retreat. Doesn't shut down.

And that—God. That matters.

It feels like the first fault line in the fortress he's built around himself. A hairline crack in all that control. He let me in, just a sliver, and it feels more intimate than anything he could've said out loud.

My throat closes around the ache. The gratitude. The overwhelming need to press my palm against his chest and ask —Who hurt you? Who left you bleeding and decided you had to survive alone?

But I don't.

Because this? Him offering without demand, without defense?

That's sacred ground. And I won't stomp through it just because I'm desperate for more.

So I lean into him. Rest my head against his shoulder.

Say nothing.

His arm tightens.

Just a little. A fraction.

But I feel it.

Feel it like a live current sparking beneath my skin, like a promise without words. My body goes hot and sharp and acutely aware—of the rise and fall of his chest, the scent of pine and storm and him, the heavy press of his thigh against mine.

Outside, thunder mutters low, a belly-deep growl retreating toward the horizon.

But in here, the storm is alive and well—trapped between our bodies, wound tight and waiting.

"Thank you," I whisper, barely more than breath. "For the foxes. For... this."

I gesture vaguely, helpless to explain the feeling clawing at my chest. The weight of his arm. The safety and the danger of it. The silence between us that's louder than any scream.

Caleb turns his head.

Looks at me.

Really looks.

And it's like being struck. Like a match dragged against skin. His gaze drops to my mouth and stays there, and every inch of me pulls taut. Heat coils low. My pulse skitters like prey in a snare.

I tilt my chin without thinking. Lips parting. Needing.

Needing him.

The air crackles, thick with everything we haven't said. With want. With hesitation. With the kind of pull that lives in bone and instinct, not reason.

His head dips.

Breath brushes my lips. Tastes like rain and restraint.

I forget how to breathe.

My eyes flutter shut—

CRACK!

A deafening crash overhead.

The hut jolts.

We tear apart like we've been struck by lightning, adrenaline and lust crashing together in a jarring, breathless snap.

He stands fast, scanning the roof.

I press a hand to my chest, heart racing like I just jumped out of a plane.

The storm's still out there.

But the one between us?

It's only getting started.

My heart, which just moments ago had been cartwheeling from the almost-kiss, now jackhammers against my ribs like it's trying to claw its way out. Caleb's already moving—fluid, focused, scanning the ceiling with a soldier's precision. Every muscle in his body wired and ready.

"Branch," he says, voice flat. "Deadfall from the upper tree line."

Like we weren't seconds away from tearing into each

other. Like I wasn't just about to climb him and beg him to ruin me.

I'm still catching my breath, still trying to reboot every system that short-circuited the second his mouth hovered over mine. He's checking the roof for leaks. Leaks. As if we didn't just shatter the atmosphere between us.

The moment's gone.

Snuffed out like a candle between two fingers.

But the heat?

Still burns. Low and fierce beneath my skin. Curling in my belly. Thrumming between my legs.

He moves to the window and clears his throat, voice neutral again. "Storm's passing. We should head back before the next system hits."

I nod, because words are currently a foreign language. Outside, the storm has dulled to a steady patter. I shrug out of the blanket, fingers trembling, and grab my camera, checking that it's dry under my jacket.

We don't talk on the hike back. We don't have to. The silence between us is thick with all the things we almost did. All the things we still want to do.

By the time the ranger cabin comes into view, I'm soaked again. Rain runs down my spine in cold, shivery streams. My clothes cling in all the wrong places. Caleb reaches the porch first, holds the door for me.

I step inside.

Then stop.

We're standing just inside the cabin, dripping onto the floor, steam rising off our skin as warm air meets cold rain.

And he looks like every dark, primal fantasy I've ever had.

His shirt is soaked, transparent, molded to every cut and line of muscle. His chest rises and falls like he's barely holding it together. And when our eyes meet—

That's it.

The air splits.

No warning. No hesitation.

He moves.

One second of stillness, and then he's on me—closing the distance in two strides like a storm bearing down. His hand comes up—rough, calloused, his—and it's on my face, cupping my jaw with a kind of reverent urgency that steals the breath from my lungs. His palm is warm despite the chill, fingers splayed across my cheek, thumb brushing the corner of my mouth like he's trying to memorize the shape of it.

His touch is unsteady. Controlled and shaking. Like he's fighting every instinct and losing all at once.

He tilts my chin up, dragging my gaze to his. And what I see there? It's not restraint anymore. It's hunger. Desperation. Raw, soul-deep ache. Like I'm the first light after a lifetime in shadow. Like he's drowning and I'm the only thing keeping him above the surface.

And then—God.

Then his mouth crashes down on mine.

No prelude. No gentleness. Just fire. Just need.

The kiss is feral. Consuming. Like he's trying to drink me in, devour every second we've denied this. It's teeth and tongue and heat, the press of his body against mine, the scrape of stubble against my skin, the taste of rain and restraint snapping clean in half.

He kisses like he's furious it took this long.

Like I'm the only thing that's ever made sense—and he doesn't trust it.

My hands fist in his shirt, yanking him closer, anchoring myself to the storm that is him. His other arm wraps around my waist, iron-tight, hauling me flush against his chest like he's afraid I'll vanish. There's nothing careful in him now. No holding back. Just a silent ache turned kinetic.

My spine hits the nearest wall, and I gasp against his

mouth—he swallows it whole, groaning low, deep in his throat, a sound so primal it makes my knees buckle.

We kiss like we've already fallen.

Like we're already burning.

Like if we stop—we won't survive it.

There's no hesitation. No caution. Just heat. Hunger. Possession.

His lips are like fire against mine, his tongue sweeping into my mouth like he owns it—like he's finally claiming what he's been denying himself since the moment we met. I moan into him, clutching his shirt, trying to pull him closer. Trying to feel all of him, the press and burn and stretch of him against me.

He groans—low and raw, vibrating between our bodies.

One arm wraps around my waist, yanking me into him like he can't stand even an inch of space. The other buries in my hair, angling my head, deepening the kiss until I can't breathe, don't want to.

His hips drive into mine, all heat and hardness, and it's like a match to gasoline. I grind against him, desperate for friction, for pressure, for more.

My shirt sticks when he tries to yank it up—wet cotton refusing to move.

He growls, frustrated, tries again.

Still stuck.

We both are.

Caught in this inferno, clinging to each other like the world might end, and this is all we get.

Then he pulls back.

Just enough to rest his forehead against mine. His breath comes fast. Shaky.

"Fuck." His voice is wrecked. "This isn't... I shouldn't have—"

I don't move.

Because I need him to finish. To say something real. To undo or redo what we just did. Anything but leave me hanging here, scorched and shaking.

His hands still rest on my waist. Fingers twitching like he doesn't want to let go.

But he does.

Steps back, slow and careful, like I'm made of fire and he's already burned.

His hands lift. Palms up. Fingers spread.

Not surrender.

Distance.

"I'm sorry," he rasps, voice frayed. "That... shouldn't have happened."

But his eyes say the opposite.

His eyes say it had to happen.

His chest rises with a sharp breath—like the air's been punched out of him and he's only now realizing he needs it back. But he doesn't look at me. Not directly. Not after what just happened.

Not after we both let something dangerous and unspeakably real crack open between us like lightning splitting a centuries-old pine.

"You need to get out of those clothes," he says, backing up another step like I'm the one on fire.

"I'm not—"

"You're soaked." Too fast. Too sharp. He's not talking about the rain. "Body temp drops fast in this altitude. Hypothermia isn't something I want on your list."

My list.

Right. Stranded. Bruised. Heartsick. And apparently one steamy kiss away from sending a battle-hardened ranger into full retreat.

"I'll grab you dry clothes. Start the fire," he adds, already moving like a man fleeing an ambush. "There's a towel in the cabinet. Use it. And get under the blankets."

"Caleb—wait—" My voice catches, tangled with everything I want to ask. Want to feel again.

But he's already at the door. His hand on the knob. Rain slants behind him in silver sheets, catching the porchlight like static.

"I need to check the water line," he says, voice low. Distant. "Make sure the runoff didn't wash anything out.

Bullshit.

We both know it.

The storm can wait.

I can't.

"Caleb."

He stops.

One hand pressed against the doorframe. Shoulders tight. Jaw clenched. His head bows like he's praying for control.

"I just need..." His voice scrapes out of him, low and rough. "I just need a minute."

And then he's gone.

The door shuts behind him with a sound that feels like a slammed heartbeat.

And suddenly the room is too quiet. Too still. Too empty.

The fire hasn't been lit yet, but the heat that filled this space only moments ago is already gone—dragged out into the storm with him. I stand there, heart pounding, body humming, lips still aching from the memory of his mouth on mine.

And the silence he left behind wraps around me like smoke.

Not warmth.

Just the echo of a man who kissed me like he couldn't stop...

Then ran like he had to get away.

I'm left standing there, heart pounding, lips still tingling from the kiss I never saw coming but can't stop reliving. The air he leaves behind feels cold and expansive, as if the room has forgotten how to hold heat once he walked out of it.

Angel's Peak

CHAPTER 8

Sleep is a joke.

I spend most of the night tangled in damp sheets and worse thoughts—replaying that kiss on an endless loop. The heat of his mouth. The bite of his fingers digging into my waist. The way he kissed me like he was starving, and I was the only thing left to feed on.

I analyze every breath, every flick of his tongue, every sound that escaped me. And reach exactly zero conclusions.

Except that I want it again.

Desperately.

Dangerously.

By the time I crawl out of the cot, it's late morning and the fire's burned low. Caleb stands at the stove, back rigid, broad shoulders tense beneath clean flannel. Not the same one from yesterday. That one was soaked through, clinging to every sculpted inch of him like sin

This one hides more, and somehow, that only makes it worse.

He doesn't turn as I cross the room. Doesn't speak. His

jaw ticks when I approach. And his grip on the handle of the pan tightens.

"Morning," I say, aiming for breezy. It lands somewhere around breathless and achy.

"Coffee's ready."

Flat.

Neutral.

Like we didn't nearly combust last night.

I pour myself a mug, deliberately avoiding the memory of how he tasted—rain, pine, heat.

SIN!

The silence stretches between us like a live wire. Yesterday we found something easy. Quiet, yes—but companionable. Today, that silence feels barbed and threatening.

"Thanks for showing me the foxes." I settle onto a stool across from him. "Got some great shots."

"Good." He nods, still not meeting my eyes.

One word. One syllable.

A fucking brick wall.

I can't take it. "About what happened—"

"Eggs are ready." He slides a plate in front of me, cutting me off with more force than necessary. A thin crack echoes through the air as the ceramic plate meets wood.

Right.

Back to strictly nutritional exchanges.

Got it, Mountain Man.

We eat in silence, forks scraping across our plates, the rain ticking softly against the windows like it's trying to fill the space between us.

His flannel is dry, his expression unreadable. I'm still damp somewhere under my skin, still burned from the inside out. He doesn't look at me once.

Whatever that kiss meant to him, it's been filed away. Locked up. Dismissed.

After breakfast, I escape to the window seat and pretend I'm deeply invested in reviewing my photos. In truth, I barely register the images. My skin still remembers the press of his hands. My mouth aches with phantom hunger. My thoughts are all static and heat.

Across the room, Caleb moves with the relentless focus of a man trying very hard not to think. He rifles through paperwork like it personally offends him. Tension pulses off him like a second storm system inside the cabin.

We're both pretending nothing happened.

Neither of us is convincing.

And the worst part?

I miss the man who couldn't keep his hands off me.

When I can't stand the silence—or the thrum of memory still echoing on my lips—I abandon my camera and drift through the cabin like a ghost with nowhere to haunt. The space feels smaller today, like it's pressing in, thick with everything we're not saying.

I trail my fingers over the worn spines of books, mostly wilderness manuals and fire science texts, each neatly arranged. Maps cover one wall, edges curled with age and use, marked in red ink and tightly printed notes. His handwriting is clean, controlled, and repressed, just like him.

And then I see it.

A small wooden box tucked on a shelf near the fireplace. It's too beautiful to belong here—carved with delicate patterns that don't match the rest of the cabin's rugged utility.

It looks... loved.

Kept.

I reach for it without thinking, fingertips grazing the polished lid.

It slips before I even know I've moved it wrong.

Crack!

The sound is too sharp, too final. Like a bone snapping. Or a promise breaking.

I freeze. The box is on the floor, the lid split clean off, a burst of tiny glass shards glittering like fallen stars across the rug.

Caleb's across the room in the blink of an eye—no words, just motion, fast and sharp. He drops to his knees and gathers the broken pieces with trembling hands.

I take a step forward—

"I'm so sorry," I say quickly, heat surging into my face. "I didn't mean—"

"Don't touch it." His voice lashes out like a whip. Cold. Controlled.

Meant to sting.

I freeze again. Hands up, stepping back like I'm the one who's broken.

He cradles a shattered ornament in his palm—what looks like a bird, or maybe it used to be. The curve of a wing, a fragment of a beak. It's beautiful, even in ruin.

"It was an accident," I say, softer now. "Caleb... I didn't know—"

"You shouldn't have been touching it." His voice stays low, but the fury in it vibrates the air. "This isn't a tourist attraction. These aren't souvenirs."

"I know that." I swallow, guilt twisting sharply in my stomach. "I—I just—It stood out. I was curious. I'll pay to fix it."

"Some things can't be fixed." He stands abruptly, chest rising with ragged restraint, the broken box still clutched in one hand. His knuckles have gone bloodless.

It's not about the ornament. That much is obvious.

The pain in his voice is the kind that's settled deep in bone and refuses to heal. My apology stalls in my throat, useless in the face of whatever memory I just callously cracked open like the box on the floor.

"Who was she?" The question slips out—quiet, but sharp enough to cut.

His head jerks up. His eyes lock on mine, and for a second, I forget how to breathe.

"What?"

"The redhead," I say, gently. "In the photo by your desk. She's the one who gave you the box, isn't she?"

The silence that follows isn't just tense. It's suffocating.

I half-expect him to throw me out into the rain.

But he doesn't. His face just... folds inward. Shutters down. It's painful to watch.

Something fragile presses behind his eyes.

"Kim." The name scrapes out of him like it costs something. "She was our team's meteorologist. Weather specialist."

Was.

The word thuds through the room like a dropped weight.

"She's...she's the one who died," I murmur, the full picture clicking into place. "She was your—"

"My fiancée."

The word is final. Flat.

It lands in my chest with a jolt of pain so real it steals my breath. Oh.

This is what he's been holding back. Not just a tragedy. Not just the fire. But her. A future he lost in flame and ash.

"Caleb..." My voice breaks around the edges. "I'm so sorry. I didn't know."

"I know you didn't." He turns away, setting the broken box down with aching care. His hands linger there longer than necessary, knuckles still taut, breath shallow.

The silence after is unbearable. Not just awkward now—exposed.

And beneath the ache, something dangerous coils low in my belly. Not just because of the pain I saw on his face. But because I felt it. And I want to be the one who reaches past that barricade he's so carefully constructed.

That's the worst possible impulse, isn't it?

I broke something that mattered, yet here I stand, terrified that I want to break more. I want to break through his walls. Watch them crumble. For me.

Not a ghost in his past.

"Sierra Station, this is Dispatch. Do you copy?"

He moves to the radio as it crackles to life, effectively ending the conversation.

"Sierra Station. Go ahead." His voice betrays none of the emotion I just witnessed.

"Update on road conditions. Landslide on the main access road. Estimate minimum five additional days before clearing crews can get through. Do you have adequate supplies?"

Five more days. The news should distress me—more time stranded away from civilization, away from my assignment. Instead, I feel a treacherous flutter of something like relief.

"Need to check inventory." Caleb glances my way. "Will report back within the hour."

"Copy that. Dispatch out."

He turns to me, professional mask firmly in place. "I need to count supplies."

"Do you want help?"

"Sure." From the way his shoulders droop, it's clear I'm the last person he wants helping him. Me, the one who snooped. Me, the one who broke something precious to him.

We work in tense silence, cataloging food stores, water reserves, fuel for the generator, and other essentials. The mundane task keeps our hands busy while the unspoken hovers between us—his revelation, our kiss, the uncertain dynamic that shifts like quicksand beneath our feet.

"Enough food for two weeks, if we're careful." He makes notes in a small ledger. "Water filtration system is working, so that's not a concern."

"What about power?"

"Generator has enough fuel for emergencies. Solar panels handle basic needs when there's sun." He checks another cabinet. "Propane for cooking is sufficient."

The inventory takes us to a storage closet I hadn't noticed before, tucked beside the back bedroom. Inside, shelves hold neatly organized supplies—everything from medical kits to spare blankets. One corner contains what appears to be a small workshop, with carving tools arranged on a pegboard and several blocks of wood in various stages of completion.

I pick up a partially carved figure—a fox, its features emerging from the wood with remarkable detail. "You made this?"

Caleb hesitates before nodding. "Helps pass the time."

"It's beautiful." I examine another piece—an owl with intricately textured feathers. "You're talented."

"Just a hobby." He takes the carving from my hands, setting it back on the shelf.

"The box—the one I broke. You made that too?"

Pain flickers across his face. "Yes."

"I really am sorry." I meet his eyes, willing him to believe my sincerity.

"I know." Something in his expression softens fractionally. "I shouldn't have snapped at you. I'm sorry I snapped."

"I deserved it. It was my fault. I was bored and careless. I broke something precious to you, and I am really sorry about that."

This small concession eases the tension between us. As we finish the inventory, conversation flows more naturally, focusing on practical matters without the earlier strain.

When we return to the main room, Caleb crosses to the

radio and checks in with Dispatch to confirm supplies and status. His voice is steady and professional—there is no trace of what happened just minutes ago, and there is no hint that anything inside him might be unraveling.

When the call ends, he turns to the broken box gently, like it might still feel pain.

His fingers trace the fracture, thumb brushing the splintered edge with reverence that punches straight through my ribs. Not for the wood. For what it represents.

"Can it be repaired?" I ask, hovering close enough to feel the tension radiating off him.

"The box, yeah." He doesn't look up. "The glass bird? No."

"What kind of bird was it?"

"Golden eagle." His eyes flick to mine, and in that moment, the air shifts. He doesn't say it like he's naming a species—he says it like he's naming a ghost. "Kim studied their nesting patterns. Focused on fire zones."

The breath catches in my throat.

That's why he knew where to find the nesting sites. That's why he moved through those woods like they whispered to him.

"You've been continuing her work," I say quietly, but it lands between us like thunder. "Like I'm finishing my father's."

His nod is slow. Controlled. But his hands tighten around the damaged box like he can hold the past together with sheer force of will.

Something opens between us. Not just shared grief—purpose. The same hollow ache of wanting to give meaning to what was stolen.

"Why did you kiss me?" The words tumble out before I can stop them.

Angel's Peak

CHAPTER 9

Caleb's hands go still.

The silence that follows could shatter glass. He sets the box down like it's suddenly radioactive. Like touching it any longer might burn.

"I shouldn't have." His voice is low. Flat. A forced calm that doesn't match the storm behind his eyes. "It won't happen again."

"That's not what I asked."

His entire body goes rigid. And then, like it costs him, he takes a slow step back. One pace. Two. Like putting space between us might scrub away what we both felt.

"It's the only answer that matters."

"Bullshit."

The word snaps through the air—sharp, jagged, louder than I meant it. But I don't take it back. I won't.

"You wanted it. I wanted it. So what's the real problem, Caleb? Because it didn't feel like a mistake. It felt like the only damn thing in this cabin that made sense."

He exhales through his nose, slow and controlled, like I'm a wildfire and he's trying not to fan the flames.

"The problem is we're stuck in close quarters. Cut off from reality. Running on adrenaline and isolation and goddamn ghost stories. That kind of pressure warps things. Makes people do things they wouldn't normally do."

He says it like he's reading from a manual. Like he's trying to convince himself.

My pulse thrums like a warning drum. I step closer. The space he created? I take it back.

"Is that what you're clinging to?" My voice drops, low and steady. "That it was the storm? The cold? Some survival instinct? Tell yourself whatever you want—but don't you dare lie to me."

"It's not a lie." Grit lines his voice now. "It's the truth."

"No," I whisper, stepping closer. "It's fear."

His jaw flexes. I see it. That little tick at the corner where he clenches too hard. He doesn't deny it.

"You felt something. You're just scared of it. That kiss—it wasn't a fluke. It wasn't proximity or bad timing or some kind of emotional mirage. It was real. And it scared the hell out of you."

He stares at me like I'm a fault line beneath his feet, and he doesn't know whether to step forward or run.

"You think you're the only one who's lost someone? You think you've cornered the damn market on grief?" My voice cracks, the words scraping raw. "You think shutting down makes you strong? It doesn't. It makes you a coward."

The air pulls taut. He's not breathing. Neither am I.

Then, finally—his voice, low and ragged, just above a whisper.

"I'm not afraid of kissing you."

"Then what are you afraid of?" I press, barely holding myself together. "Me? Or what it would mean if it wasn't just a kiss?"

His gaze drops. Not to retreat. But because the answer's already written behind his eyes—and it's tearing him apart.

He looks away like he's trying to protect me. Or maybe trying to protect himself. From me. From what this is. From what it could be.

And that? That hurts more than if he'd shoved me out the damn door.

Because if he yelled, if he snapped, if he let something—anything—break through that iron self-control, at least I'd know where we stand. But this?

This is a slow collapse. A quiet retreat. And retreat always comes before abandonment.

My chest tightens. That sharp, breath-stealing ache creeps in. The one I know too well. The one that screams he's leaving before he's even gone.

"You are scared." I don't move back. I move closer. Right into his space. Right where it hurts. "Not of me. Of what I represent. Connection. Possibility. Something that might crack open the walls you've bricked yourself behind."

His jaw ticks again, tighter this time. He grits his teeth. "Two days, and you think you've figured me out?"

"I know enough." My voice trembles. But I don't back off. "You're kind even when you pretend not to be. You'd rather freeze than let someone else be cold. You care about every fox den and broken pine on this mountain like they're yours to protect. And you kissed me like you've been starving for something real. Like I was your first breath after years underwater."

"Stop." The word grates out of him like it hurts to say. Like it costs too much.

"No."

He steps back.

I follow.

"That kiss," I whisper, eyes burning, heart pounding, "was real. Maybe the only real thing you've let yourself feel in years.

And you're terrified of what it means if you let yourself want more."

His breath shudders. One hand clenches at his side.

But he doesn't deny it.

And that silence? That silence says everything.

We're close now. Too close.

Breathing the same damp, electric air. His chest rises and falls like he's just come down off a sprint, though neither of us is moving. His gaze locks with mine, dark and dangerous, pupils blown wide.

The air crackles—alive with the kind of charge that lives in the sky before lightning strikes.

"You're leaving in a matter of days." His voice drops, gravelly rough. "Then it's back to your life. Planes, continents, chasing light through a lens."

"So?" My voice is low, defiant.

"So this—" his hand slices the air between us, "—doesn't end well. We start something here, it only ends with regret."

"Who said anything about happy endings?" I take a step closer, heat rising up my throat like a fever. "Maybe this isn't about later. Maybe it's just about now."

His jaw clenches.

And for a heartbeat, I think he'll cave.

Then the radio crackles.

Static slices the moment. Caleb spins toward it like it's a lifeline, not a fucking excuse. His hands move with too much force, twisting the knob, adjusting the frequency with the kind of precision that only comes from needing something to control.

By the time he turns back, he's hiding behind that damn mask again. The one carved from stone and silence.

But his shoulders are too tight. His hands too still. He won't meet my eyes.

"It's for your own good," he says.

"Don't." My voice sharpens, rage cutting through the heat. "Don't you dare pull that patronizing bullshit. I'm not a porcelain doll. I'm a grown woman who knows exactly what she wants."

He moves.

One step.

Then another.

Until his chest nearly brushes mine.

His control slips. It shows in the tightness around his mouth, the heat bleeding from his skin, the hunger vibrating off him in waves.

"You don't understand," he growls, voice fraying. "I don't just want you." His breath hits my cheek. Hot. Shaking. "I want to take you apart."

Lightning arcs down my spine. My breath stutters.

"I want to hear the pitch of your breath when I pin your wrists above your head and make you beg," he grits out. "I want your thighs trembling when I bury my face between them. I want you whispering my name like a prayer and cursing me when I don't let you come until you're half-wild."

My knees weaken. I grip the edge of the table behind me to stay upright.

He steps closer—just enough for his voice to go quiet, deadly.

"I want you bent over the damn boulder behind the shelter," he rasps. "Your pants shoved down, your ass red from my hand before I take you so deep you forget who you are."

My mouth opens. No sound comes.

"And that's just the beginning."

His voice lowers even further, rough and raw, like he hates himself for this—like he needs me to hate him for it.

"I want your mouth full of me, your eyes wet, your throat raw from how deep I fuck you. I want to hold your head in my hands and make you take every inch while you gag, choke, and beg for more."

A helpless sound slips out of me—high, broken, wanting.

"I'll hurt you," he warns, barely audible now. "Not because I want to break you. But because I don't know how to do anything less than everything. I don't do soft. I don't do careful."

He leans in, lips a breath from mine, his voice shaking with restraint.

"Is that what you want?"

"Caleb..." My voice is wrecked.

"No." His fingers curl into fists. "You started this. I'm just telling you the truth. I want you wrecked. Raw. I want to see my handprint on your skin, my name in your mouth, your legs shaking from how hard you came on my cock."

I shake with the force of how badly I want him. How badly I want that.

"God, yes," I whisper, fire licking up my spine. "If you knew the things I've imagined you doing to me... you wouldn't be trying so damn hard to hold back."

He growls—growls—low and primal, like he's two seconds from snapping the last thread of control he has.

And God help us both when he does.

"Like what?" His voice scrapes through the tension like a blade—low, rough, already unraveling, and then his gaze sharpens, as if I've sucker punched him straight in the restraint.

"You want to know what I want?"

"Yes."

"Do you?"

"For the love of God..." His jaw ticks, like he's about to combust.

"The tree behind the fox shelter." My voice barely carries

over the pounding of my pulse. "The way it curves just right... Every time I saw it, I pictured you pressing me against the bark. My wrists tangled in vines. Your mouth everywhere."

His breath hitches.

My lips are too dry to speak, but I do. Because now that the dam has cracked, there's no stopping this flood. My body is aching and ready... for him.

"I've pictured you taking me against nearly every tree out there. Bark tearing my jacket. One hand on my throat, the other locked around my hip—holding me in place while you fuck me like you need it. Like you'd die if you didn't."

"Fuck." The word explodes from his mouth, guttural and harsh, like it rips something loose inside him.

"I'm not done." My voice is trembling, desperate, unashamed. "That boulder behind the shed—your hand, my ass. I want that. I need that. I want your control. Your craving. Your edge. I want all fifty shades of your darkness and everything beyond. Don't hold back for me."

His whole body vibrates with tension. His hands clench into fists, jaw rigid, chest heaving.

"It's like someone carved you out of sin and stubbornness," he mutters, voice low and ruined, "and dropped you on my porch just so I could break you open."

"Maybe." My knees go weak. The air between us pulses like it's alive.

His hand twitches. Once. Twice. Like he's seconds from giving in.

"There's a boulder at the overlook," I say, breath hitched, heart in my throat. "Every time we passed it, I imagined you bending me over it. One hand holding me down, the other wrapped in my hair while I scream your name into the wind."

His head tips back like he's in pain. His throat works once. Twice. Then his gaze drops to mine—feral. Starved.

"Jesus Christ." It's not a prayer. It's a warning.

He stares at me like I've torn something open inside him.

I take one step closer.

"You want to dominate me?" My voice is hoarse, rough with need. "Then stop talking about it and do it."

His restraint shatters.

He lunges.

One second of stillness—then chaos. His hands grip my face like he's drowning, his mouth crashing onto mine with zero finesse and absolute need. I gasp, and he takes it—drinks it down like it's oxygen.

Then he spins me, slams me back against the wall, not hard, but hard enough to make my breath catch.

"Tell me to stop," he growls against my lips.

"No."

"Tell me you can take it."

"I can take it."

His hands are everywhere—at my hips, up under my shirt, dragging a moan from my throat as he presses every hard inch of his body against mine. There's no space left. No oxygen. No sanity.

"Caleb—"

His name is a gasp, a plea, a spark.

He bites my lower lip, then kisses the sting like an apology he doesn't mean. His fingers thread into my hair and tug my head back, forcing my gaze to his.

"You wanted wrecked?" His voice is a vow now. "You're about to be fucking ruined."

He's on me, his mouth crashing into mine, nothing gentle, nothing soft. Just raw, hungry, carnal need. His hands are on my hips, dragging me into him, pressing me against the wall.

I gasp into the kiss and he growls, deep in his throat, a sound that says he's seconds from losing control completely.

But he doesn't.

The kiss is brutal, hot, and deep, and utterly consuming.

His mouth crashes into mine with enough force to drive me back against the wall. His hands grip my hips like he's afraid I'll disappear, like I'm the only thing anchoring him to this earth.

I moan into him, helpless and greedy, as his thigh wedges between mine, grinding upward, forcing a cry from my throat. One of his hands slides up my torso, fingers curling around my throat—not tight, just there—a promise.

And I arch into it.

"Say it." He pulls back just enough to look at me—really look. His breathing is ragged. His pupils are blown wide.

"I need you to fuck me," I whisper.

His eyes search mine. Something unspoken trembles between us. His hands fist my shirt. The damp fabric clinging to his calloused palms, and then—he stops.

Just... stops.

His whole body shakes like he's hanging on by a thread.

"Fuck," he grits out. "You have no idea what you're asking." A tremor rolls through his arms like he's shaking from the effort of holding himself back.

"I do." My lips brush his. "You don't scare me. Not even a little."

His next breath is sharp, brutal. He steps back, his muscles shaking, and his breath ragged. One hand drags over his mouth like he's wiping away the taste of what he almost did.

"Caleb?" I can barely get the name out. "What—"

"I can't." His eyes squeeze shut. When he speaks, his voice is shredded.

"Why not?"

"Because if I touch you now, I won't stop. I won't be gentle. I won't slow down or ask questions or check in." He looks at me, wrecked and raw. "And I can't risk that. Not with you."

"You think you'll hurt me?"

"I *know* I will."

And there it is—the fracture line beneath all that mountain steel.

He isn't scared of wanting me.

He's terrified he'll break me.

"I need air," he says, voice broken. "I need to go before I hurt you without meaning to."

I reach for him, but he shakes his head, already grabbing his jacket.

"Get out of those wet clothes or you'll get hypothermic," he mutters, not looking at me. "There's a blanket by the stove. I'll check the water line."

And just like that—he's gone.

But this time, it's not a retreat.

It's restraint. The kind forged in fire and beaten into bone.

Because even a man built from granite knows when to stop.

Because real control doesn't come from taking—it comes from knowing when not to.

When he comes back, storm-washed and steel-eyed, boots heavy with mud and decision... He won't hesitate.

He'll take.

He'll strip me bare like bark from a tree, bend me over anything that'll hold my weight, and make me beg until I forget my name.

Not out of anger.

Out of hunger.

And I'm done pretending I want anything less than to be wrecked by him—mind, body, and every aching inch in between.

Let the mountain bear witness.

Next time, I won't be the one trembling.

I'll be the one begging him not to stop.

I press myself into the corner of the window seat like it

might anchor me, trying to make sense of the chaos he left behind. My heart pounds. My thoughts snarl, too tangled to unravel, too loud to silence.

The rain continues its steady patter against the glass, amplifying the charged silence in the cabin.

Somewhere out there, he waits.

Angel's Peak

CHAPTER 10

The scent of baking bread drags me from sleep—thick, yeasty, primal. It curls through the ranger station like temptation, sweet and slow, wrapping itself around my senses and tugging me out of dreams I'm not ready to leave.

Dreams where Caleb's hands aren't just holding me... they're claiming me. Pinning me. Tearing me apart in the most delicious ways.

For a moment, I lie still, soaked in warmth, pretending the ache in my core is from his mouth on my skin, not some phantom memory I'm burning to make real. But the smell—it won't let me linger. It pulls at me, relentless and tender all at once.

Like him.

I throw on jeans and a sweater. My fingers rake through my hair, but nothing tames the wildness inside me. Not after last night. Not after what we said. What we didn't do.

My bare feet hit the floor. I pad into the main room—and freeze.

Caleb stands at the counter, sleeves shoved up, forearms

dusted with flour. He kneads dough with strong hands, each movement controlled, focused, almost meditative.

Calloused hands. Strong hands. Dangerous hands.

The same ones that pinned me to the wall like a promise.

A loaf cools beside him, golden and perfect. The whole scene is wrong—he's too big, too dangerous, too raw for this kind of gentleness.

I want all of him, but nothing about him is safe.

He's all coiled muscle and tension, too big, too raw for the softness of warm bread and honeyed silence. The contrast slices through me, sharp and aching. I want to taste it. All of it. The gentleness. The violence. The way he makes me feel like a live wire stretched too tight.

His gaze lifts, locks with mine.

Snap.

Electricity explodes between us, wild and hungry and unspoken. His nod is casual, but his eyes? His eyes are pure heat. Remembering. Imagining. Needing.

"Morning." His voice scrapes low and rough, still thick with sleep and something darker. "Coffee's ready."

"You bake?" My voice comes out breathless, incredulous, betraying too much.

A flush climbs his neck. "Supply runs are limited. Easier to make my own." He looks away, but not before I catch the way his jaw tightens, the way his eyes flick over me—quick, assessing, hungry. Like he's remembering the words I moaned into the dark. And wishing he'd answered them with action.

I pour coffee, hands trembling just enough to betray me. I watch him work, the flex of his forearms, the way his fingers sink into the dough. I remember those hands on my skin, the way he held me against the wall, the way he stopped—barely.

"Where'd you learn?" I ask, needing to fill the silence, needing to hear his voice.

"My grandmother." He rinses his hands, muscles shifting

beneath his shirt. "She believed every person should know how to create something essential." He grabs a towel, dries his hands slow. Controlled.

His words hang between us, loaded. I wonder if he's thinking about what else he could create with those hands—what he could destroy.

"Bread is pretty essential." My voice drops, teasing—but there's an edge beneath it. Hunger, hot and sharp.

That mouth of his curves. Not a full smile—just a flicker. Dangerous. Male. Heat simmers just below the surface.

"That was her point." His eyes linger, heat simmering just beneath the surface. "Hungry?"

For you. The words almost slip out. Instead, I nod, pulse thudding in my throat.

He slices the loaf, the knife gliding through the crust with a satisfying crackle. He adds butter, honey, apples—each movement precise, deliberate, as if he needs the ritual to keep his hands busy, to keep from reaching for me.

Like it's the only thing stopping him from crossing the room and backing me against the wall again.

I sit, trying not to squirm under the weight of his gaze. I try to breathe normally. Try to ignore the way his forearms flex with every slice. I try to ignore how his shoulders strain under his shirt.

"What's the occasion?" My voice is thin, a little too high. My voice is too high. Too light. Like I'm pretending this is normal.

"Weather's breaking." He nods toward the window, sunlight streaming through the thinning clouds. "Radio says we've got a clear window today before the next system moves in."

"So we're not stuck inside all day?" I can't hide the relief—or the disappointment. I want out of these four walls, but I want him to stop pretending we're safe from each other.

He hesitates, then, softer, "Thought I might show you something. If you're interested."

His words are loaded, heavy with everything we didn't finish last night. I see the storm in his eyes, the restraint stretched thin, ready to snap. I want to push him. I want to see what happens when he finally lets go.

I meet his gaze, let him see the hunger in my eyes. "I'm interested."

His breath catches, just for a second. The tension between us hums—thick, electric, impossible to ignore. The air tastes like bread and coffee and longing.

I could push him. One word. One touch. One breath too close.

But not yet.

Let him simmer.

Let him suffer.

Let him burn.

He looks away, jaw clenched, fighting for control. I see the tremor in his hands as he sets the knife down, as he pours honey over the bread. I want to lick it from his fingers. I want to ruin him right back.

We eat in silence, every bite charged, every glance a dare. I wonder if he's thinking about pinning me to the table, about taking me apart piece by piece, about making good on every filthy promise he made last night.

When he finally stands, the chair scraping back, the heat of his gaze blisters my skin. He holds out a hand, steady, but his knuckles are white.

"Come," he says, voice rough with everything he isn't saying. "Let's go."

And I follow, heart pounding, already burning for the storm I know is coming.

"Where?"

"Something you'll enjoy."

"The eagle nesting site?" I can't quite hide the eagerness in my voice. Not after last night. Not after the way his hands left invisible fingerprints on my skin.

He nods, sliding a plate toward me. "Need to check it anyway. Trail might be rough after the rain."

I take a bite of bread, eyes fluttering closed. The crust shatters beneath my teeth, yielding to a pillowy, tangy center. I moan before I can stop myself.

"This is incredible."

That almost-smile flickers across his mouth, heat banked but not hidden. "Sourdough. Starter's over five years old."

"Something else you brought with you when you left the firefighting crew?"

He nods, gaze dropping to his plate. "One of the few things." His voice is softer, the usual edge replaced by something quieter, more honest. There's no wall between us now, only the faint, unspoken ache of restraint.

We eat in a silence that feels intimate, not awkward. Every brush of his hand, every accidental glance, sends a ripple of heat through me. When we finish, he packs water, food, and emergency gear. I gather my camera, pulse already quickening at the thought of being alone with him in the wild.

Outside, the world is scrubbed clean. Sunlight glances off rain-soaked pines, droplets clinging to needles like jewels. The air is cool, alive, scented with earth and resin and something wild.

"This way." His voice is low, steady. He leads us onto a different trail, heading up toward a rocky outcropping. "About two miles. Gets steep."

I fall in behind him, watching the way he moves—confident, sure-footed, every muscle working beneath his shirt. He owns this landscape, and I want to know what it feels like to be owned by him, even for a heartbeat.

"How'd you find this place?" I ask, needing to hear his voice, needing to keep the connection alive.

"Kim showed me." He says her name without flinching, glancing back to check on me. "She mapped every eagle nest in the range. Taught me how to read the signs."

"And you kept up her work," I say it softly, but it lands between us like a secret.

He pauses at a fallen log, offering his hand. His grip is warm, calloused, steadying me as I climb over. The contact is brief, but it leaves a trail of fire up my arm. For a moment, I imagine those hands pinning me again, rough and gentle all at once.

"The eagles mate for life," he says, voice roughening. "Same pair, same nest, year after year."

"Unless something happens to one of them."

He nods, pushing aside a low branch, holding it for me. "Kim tracked one male for six seasons. His mate disappeared in the third winter. He never took another. Just kept the nest alone until he stopped coming back."

His words are scientific, but the ache beneath them is unmistakable. I study his profile, the hard line of his jaw, the sadness that lingers in his eyes. He's talking about more than eagles.

The trail narrows, winding higher. Wind stirs the pines, the calls of birds echoing through the trees. We climb in silence, breath and heartbeat the only sounds between us.

A sudden movement in the brush snaps us both to attention. Caleb raises a hand, instantly alert. We freeze as a young deer steps into the open, trembling. Its leg is tangled in fishing line, blood welling around the cruel plastic.

"Poor thing." My heart twists. "Can we help?"

Caleb's gaze sharpens, assessing. "Maybe. If we move slow, don't spook it." He crouches, his voice dropping into a low, soothing hum—no words, just sound, gentle and commanding at once. The deer's trembling eases, just a little.

"I need to get behind it. Can you keep its attention? Move to the right, talk to it. Softly."

I nod, pulse thudding, and do as he says. The deer's wild eyes track me, but it doesn't bolt. I murmur nonsense, the gentlest words I can find, and Caleb moves—silent, controlled, every motion calculated to calm, not frighten.

In a blur, he's behind the fawn, hands steady, strong but careful as he restrains it. "Fishing line. My front pocket—multitool."

I scramble to obey, fingers trembling as I find the tool and snap out the tiny scissors. Together, we work—him holding the animal, me cutting the line, both of us moving as one. The fawn trembles, but doesn't fight, trusting us somehow.

When the last strand falls away, Caleb checks the wound, hands gentle as he applies antiseptic. The deer's breathing slows, eyes wide and dark.

"Will it be okay?" My voice is barely a whisper as I stroke the fawn's neck.

"Should heal clean." He eases his grip, slow and patient, letting the animal decide when to go. "Young enough to recover."

The deer hesitates, then bounds away, white tail flashing. We stay kneeling, close enough to touch, the air between us charged with something raw and bright.

"That was amazing." I turn to him, grinning, unable to hide my awe. "How did you know what to do?"

"Wildlife rescue training." He stands, offering his hand again, pulling me up with effortless strength. "Part of the job."

But there's something different in his eyes—a softness, a pride, a deep, unguarded satisfaction. In this moment, I see the man beneath the armor: fierce, protective, quietly aching for connection. I see how he cares, not just for wounded animals, but for every fragile thing that crosses his path—including me.

And somehow, that gentleness is just as intoxicating as his hunger. Maybe even more.

We continue our climb, the air between us humming with the afterglow of rescue and the promise of something more.

Conversation flows easily, with each step and shared discovery. Caleb points out wildflowers, lichen, the faint claw marks of a bear on a tree trunk—his knowledge is deep, but it's the way he speaks about this place that surprises me.

There's reverence in his voice, a quiet devotion that turns every fact into something intimate. He's not just reciting information; he's sharing a part of himself, letting me see the fierce tenderness that lives beneath his rough exterior.

The trail opens onto a rocky shelf, and the view punches the breath from my lungs. Peaks serrate the horizon, valleys spill out in endless green, and a river threads silver far below. The Colorado sky stretches blue and bottomless overhead, so vast it feels like it could swallow us whole.

"This is incredible." I reach for my camera, framing the scene, but nothing in my lens can touch the wild immensity before us.

"The eagle's nest is there." Caleb points, his arm brushing mine as he leans in. I follow his gesture to a nearly invisible tangle of sticks tucked into a distant cliff face. "Too far for a good shot without a telephoto. But if you're patient, you might catch them returning."

"I don't see any eagles." I lower the camera, searching the sky.

"They hunt midday. Should be back by afternoon." He settles on a flat boulder, unpacking sandwiches and water with the same careful hands that soothed a wild animal, that steadied me on the trail. "If you're willing to wait."

I sit beside him, our shoulders almost touching. We eat in

companionable silence, clouds drifting across the sun, shadows chasing over the valley. The world feels impossibly big, our worries suddenly small—yet the space between us is charged, every brush of his hand, every shared glance, a silent promise.

After a while, I find the courage to ask, "What happened that day? On Carson Ridge?"

He goes still, the question hanging in the air. For a long moment, I think he'll shut me out. But then he speaks, voice stripped bare. "Routine evac. Lightning fire moving fast. My crew was getting hikers out before the flames cut off the trail. We'd done it a hundred times."

I wait, sensing the weight pressing down on him.

"There was a family—tourists. Their boy got separated during the evacuation." Caleb's voice is tight, flat. Too controlled. "I doubled back to find him. Kim came, even though I told her not to."

His grip tightens around the water bottle, plastic crackling under his fingers. His knuckles go stark white.

"What happened?" Something icy slithers down my spine.

"We split up." His jaw flexes. "I should've stopped her. She said we had time, but fires don't give a damn about your confidence."

The silence stretches, brittle and sharp.

"I found the kid," he finally says. "Got him back to the rendezvous point. But the wind had shifted. The fire jumped ahead. Cut her off."

He doesn't look at me. His stare is fixed somewhere past the walls, lost in smoke and memory.

"She was behind the line." His voice breaks—just a fracture. A single fault line beneath all that granite. "She didn't make it."

The trail stretches ahead, open and endless, but it feels like the world just shrank around us. Like the trees are listening. Like the mountain itself is holding its breath.

The wind shifts, carrying the scent of pine and wet earth —but underneath it, something colder. Grief, maybe. Regret. The weight of everything he's not saying coils in the silence between us, thick as smoke.

It wraps around his shoulders like a second skin, heavy and worn. The guilt. The what-ifs. The split-second decisions that splinter into a thousand sleepless nights.

And I swear—for a moment—it's not the fire he's remembering.

It's her scream he never heard.

Her hand he never grabbed.

The part of himself he left behind in the flames.

"She trusted me to keep her safe. And I let her walk into a death trap." His voice is barely above a whisper now, but every word hits like an ember. Controlled. Precise. Devastating. "She died because I wasn't enough."

I reach for his hand, covering it with mine. He doesn't pull away. His skin is warm, the pulse beneath my palm steady but fragile.

"You couldn't have known," I say softly.

"I should have." His voice is a raw scrape.

"Caleb." I squeeze his hand, grounding him. "That's not on you."

He lets out a shaky breath, trying for lightness. "Two years of therapy says you're right. Doesn't change the way it feels."

"So you came here."

He finally looks at me, eyes dark and open. "Seemed fitting." A beat, then he asks, "What about you? Always the wandering photographer?"

I let him change the subject, sensing he's given all he can for now. "Always loved photography. My dad's fault. The wandering came later—after my mom broke down when he left."

He listens, really listens, as I tell him about the divorce, about the ache of loving someone who always leaves, about my habit of running before anyone can run from me.

He studies me, gaze softening with understanding. "So you keep moving."

"Harder to lose what you never really claimed." I try to laugh, but it sounds hollow.

"Does it work?" he asks quietly.

I think of my empty apartment, my half-lived life. "Not really. But it's a hard habit to break."

A shadow passes overhead—a hawk, wings wide, riding the thermals. We watch it together, silent, both of us craving a freedom we've never found.

Caleb's voice is gentle, full of insight. "We make choices to protect ourselves, then forget they were choices at all."

His words settle inside me, true and sharp. Before I can answer, dark clouds gather over the peaks, storm rolling in faster than forecast.

"Storm's coming." He stands, already packing up. "We should head back."

We move quickly down the trail, the wind whipping around us, as the first fat drops of rain splatter against the rocks. By the time the cabin comes into view, thunder is echoing through the valley, the sky a bruised, boiling gray.

We make it inside just as the downpour hits, rain hammering the roof. The temperature drops, the world outside turning wild and cold. Caleb moves through the cabin, checking the windows and feeding the woodstove, his presence filling the space—protective, solid, utterly necessary.

The lights flicker, then die as thunder shakes the walls. Darkness falls, broken only by the orange glow of the fire.

Caleb lights candles, their golden light pooling in the shadows, turning the cabin into a secret world.

I settle on the rug in front of the stove, stretching my hands toward the heat. Caleb hesitates, then sits beside me, close but not quite touching. The air between us is thick with everything we haven't said.

"Thank you for today." I turn to him, firelight painting his face in gold and shadow. "For the overlook. For trusting me."

He nods, eyes reflecting the flames. "Thank you for listening. Not many people would understand."

"I think we understand each other better than we expected."

A log shifts, sparks swirling up the chimney. The flare lights his face—so strong, so guarded, yet tonight I see the man underneath: vulnerable, yearning, afraid to want.

"Today was the first time I've spoken about Kim without feeling like I'm drowning." His voice is low. "First time I brought anyone else to that overlook."

Something in me softens, aches for him. "Thank you for sharing it with me."

He looks at me, eyes dark and hungry, voice dropping to a rough whisper. "That's the problem. I want to share things with you. Things I haven't let myself want in years."

My breath catches. The distance between us shrinks to nothing.

"Is that a problem?" My voice is barely a whisper.

"Yes." His gaze pins me. "Because you're leaving. Because I built a life around not needing anyone. Because every instinct says I should keep my distance."

"And yet..." I let the words hang, an invitation, a dare.

"And yet." He exhales, surrendering. His hand lifts, hesitant, then his calloused fingers trace my cheek, gentle and reverent in the firelight. "I've spent three years keeping everyone away," he murmurs. "But I can't seem to keep myself away from you."

The storm rages outside, but in here, it's just us—heat, longing, the slow, inexorable unraveling of everything we thought we could control.

Angel's Peak

Chapter 11

Morning light slants through the cabin windows, gold and soft, striping the floor and painting my skin. I surface from sleep slowly, drifting in the warmth left by the woodstove, the hush of rain on the roof, and the solid, unfamiliar weight of an arm draped across my waist.

We fell asleep tangled together on a nest of blankets in front of the fire, conversation spinning out into the dark—no more walls, just questions and confessions, secrets traded in low voices as the storm battered the world outside.

We talked for hours, voices low in the hush of night, slipping past defenses we didn't know we were ready to drop. I learned the shape of his grief—the jagged edges he keeps hidden under muscle and silence. The tenderness threaded into his voice when he talks about the forest. The way his eyes go soft when he thinks no one's watching.

He asked about my father. My mother. The ache of never staying long enough to be left behind. I answered with truths I've never let live outside my chest.

And now, in the early hush of morning, I lie still, not wanting to break whatever spell held him here through the night. His body curls around mine like a shield, heat seeping through the thin cotton of my shirt. His breath coasts over my neck—slow, even, until it changes.

The shift is subtle. A soft inhale, then the flex of muscle. The slide of his palm over my stomach, spreading wide. Not sleep. Not chance. A choice.

My body sparks to life.

I stay perfectly still, heart pounding against his hand. I want to push back into him, grind against the hardness pressing into the curve of my ass. I want to tempt the restraint out of him, beg him to stop pretending.

"Morning." His voice is a low growl, rough with sleep and something darker. Something hungry.

I turn in his arms. His eyes are half-lidded, hair tousled, stubble shadowing the hard lines of his jaw. There's no armor here. Just heat. Just him. And me. Tangled in the aftermath of too many truths and not enough touch.

"Morning." My voice comes out breathless, pulled from somewhere low and wanting.

His thumb skims my cheek, brushing the corner of my mouth. Lingering. Watching. Waiting. My breath stutters. His gaze drops to my lips—and holds. The tension pulls taut, electric, like the air right before a storm tears open the sky.

I don't move. I can't. I'm strung tight, aching for him to break first.

His hand slips lower, thumb teasing the edge of my hip bone. Every nerve lights up. One move. One breath. That's all it would take.

The radio crackles. Loud. Abrasive. Final.

He flinches like it burned him, and the moment is gone. He rolls away, dragging the sheet with him, tucking himself behind the shield of routine. The ranger. The protector. The man who almost let himself have me.

Frustration claws through my chest. I sit up slowly, letting the cool air replace the warmth he left behind.

Last night, every word he said, every lingering touch, was a promise.

But if he's going to ruin me like he swore—if he's going to leave marks I can't hide—then he's going to have to stop holding back.

He's going to have to stop pretending I'm something he can resist.

I will beg for many things, but I won't beg for that.

Not again.

He finishes the radio call, turning to me with a wry smile. "Another tree fell on the roof overnight. I need to assess the damage."

Just like that, the fragile intimacy of morning is gone, replaced by duty, the false comfort of structure. But something's shifted. I see it in the way his hand lingers when he passes me the coffee mug, his fingers brushing mine just a second too long. In the way his gaze catches and holds, heat banked low and dangerous behind those eyes, like a fire smoldering beneath snow.

He works quickly, muscles flexing beneath his flannel as he lifts branches and climbs the ladder. When he strips off his shirt, I can't stop staring at the strength in his arms, the way his body moves—controlled, powerful, capable of so much restraint and, I suspect, so much more.

"See something interesting?" His voice startles me, but there's a knowing glint in his eyes.

Heat floods my cheeks, but I hold his gaze. "Just making sure you don't fall. I'd hate to have to drag you back inside."

"I'll try to stay upright for you." A genuine smile breaks across his face, rare and devastating.

By mid-morning, the cabin is restored, but the tension

between us is anything but settled. He checks his watch, frowning.

"Need to hike out to the weather station. The one where we..." He trails off, but I know exactly what he means.

"The one where you almost kissed me," I say quietly, letting the memory hang between us.

"Yeah. That one." He looks at me, and something dangerous flashes in his eyes.

"I'll come with you." I dare him to refuse.

He just nods, another wall crumbling.

The forest is alive after the storm—every leaf and blade of grass shining, the air sharp and clean.

We walk side by side, our shoulders brushing, and the conversation flows easily and deeply. He shows me the weather station, his passion for the work spilling over into technical explanations and quiet pride. I watch the way his hands move and the way his mouth curves when he's talking about something he loves.

I want to taste that mouth, feel those hands on my skin, and see what happens when he finally stops holding back.

"You're still saving lives without running into fires." I tease him, but my voice is soft, full of admiration.

"Different approach. Same goal." He glances at me, eyes dark.

He finishes the download and secures the equipment. I wait, heart pounding, hoping he'll finally close the distance and give in.

"Ready for the next stop?" he asks, voice low and rough, and I see the question in his eyes—see the promise of everything we could be, if only he'll let himself want it enough.

I nod, pulse thrumming, and follow him deeper into the wild, every step a silent dare: *come and get me.*

We hike to two more monitoring stations, the rhythm of our day settling into a kind of intimate choreography. Caleb works with focus and competence, and I find myself anticipating his needs before he asks—handing him tools, steadying equipment, brushing dirt from his shoulder with a touch that lingers longer than necessary.

The miles pass beneath our boots, every step winding the tension between us tighter, every shared laugh or accidental touch another spark in the dry tinder of want.

At the final station, I steady the ladder while he climbs, his body outlined against the sky, muscles flexing beneath his shirt. I can't help but watch how he moves—confident, strong, and utterly in control.

When he descends, I'm hyperaware of the nearness of his body, the heat radiating from him, the way his fingers brush mine as he closes the equipment case.

"That should do it." His voice is low, rougher than before. "Last one."

"Back to the cabin?" My voice is breathier than I intend, hope and hunger tangled in every syllable.

He shakes his head, a glint in his eyes. "One more stop." He gestures to a narrow, hidden path. "Need to check the creek. Storm might've changed the flow."

The new trail is barely a trail, forcing us to walk close together. Wet leaves and slick mud make every step a gamble, and Caleb's hand finds my waist more than once, steadying, guiding, each touch sending a jolt of electricity straight to my core.

His palm lingers, thumb stroking the bare skin exposed above my waistband, casual and possessive.

The sound of rushing water grows louder, the air thick with the scent of rain and moss and something sharper— anticipation, thick as fog. When we reach the creek, it's transformed: a wild, churning force, swollen and dangerous.

Caleb frowns, pulling out his battered notebook, lips moving silently as he surveys the swollen creek. His focus is absolute, but I barely register his words. The world narrows to the roar of water, the cold spray misting my cheeks, the wild, living pulse of the current as it churns over rocks and fallen branches.

I edge closer, boots sinking into the spongy earth. The air is sharp and electric, charged with the aftermath of the storm. My heart beats faster, in sync with the rushing water. I should be careful, but the wildness calls to something reckless inside me—the urge to see, feel, and get as close as possible.

A gust of wind lifts my hair, the scent of wet earth and pine filling my lungs. I take another step, boots squelching in the mud. The ground looks solid, but it shifts beneath my weight, a subtle give at first—a warning I ignore.

The next instant, the bank beneath my boot gives way with a sickening, silent lurch. Time slows. My balance tips, arms windmilling, a startled gasp ripping from my throat. The world tilts, the roar of the creek swelling in my ears, the cold spray biting my skin as I pitch forward, weightless for a heartbeat.

Mud slides beneath my feet. There's nothing but the wild, churning depths below, but then strong hands clamp around my belt, yanking me back from the brink. My body collides with solid muscle, the world righting itself in a dizzying rush as Caleb hauls me against his chest, his grip bruising, desperate, utterly unyielding.

We stumble together, his momentum carrying us several steps back until his spine hits a tree, anchoring us both, his arms locked tight around me.

My breath comes in ragged bursts, my heart thundering in my ears, the afterimage of the drop still burning behind my eyes. Caleb's chest heaves against my back, the heat of his body searing through my clothes, his hold fierce and unbreakable— a living barrier between me and the wild.

"That was reckless." His breath is hot against my ear,

rough with adrenaline and something darker. His voice vibrates through my bones, more growl than words. "You scared the hell out of me."

"I'm fine," I whisper, but my voice trembles—whether from the near-miss or the feel of his arms locked around me, I can't tell.

He doesn't let go. If anything, his hold tightens, one hand spread wide over my stomach, the other banded around my waist. His body cages me, heat and strength and barely-leashed hunger.

I turn in his arms, breathless, heart pounding. His eyes are dark, pupils blown, gaze fixed on my mouth. The air between us vibrates, charged and trembling, every second stretching tight as a drawn bow.

"Caleb." His name is a plea, a dare.

His jaw flexes, restraint hanging by a thread. In one swift, decisive motion, his hand closes around the back of my neck, fingers threading into my hair, grip firm and inescapable.

He yanks me closer, mouth crashing onto mine—hot, claiming, his kiss a warning and a promise all at once. His breath is rough against my lips when he finally pulls back, his forehead pressed to mine, eyes burning into me.

"Tell me to stop." The words are a low, dangerous rumble, his hand still anchoring me in place. "Tell me you don't want this."

"I won't do that." I shake my head, lips parting.

"How dark are you willing to go?"

"As dark as you need."

There's a beat of silence... then something shatters in him —control, fear, all of it swept away by the storm inside us.

His mouth crashes down on mine, savage, hungry, unrestrained, a kiss that devours, that claims. His hand tangles in my hair, tugging my head back, exposing my throat to his teeth, his tongue, his desperate, reverent worship.

I arch into him, arms winding around his neck, pressing every inch of myself against the hard length of his body. He tastes like pine and rain and the promise of everything I've been craving—rough, wild, utterly consuming. I claw at his shoulders, his flannel bunched in my fists as I pull him closer, but closer isn't enough. I want him inside me, under my skin, wrapped around every breath.

He lifts me effortlessly, pinning me between his body and the tree, his hips grinding into mine, his hand sliding beneath my shirt, fingers splaying over bare skin, hot and possessive.

The kiss turns frantic, all teeth and tongue and breathless moans, years of restraint burning away in the heat of this moment.

"You have no idea," he growls against my mouth, biting my lower lip hard enough to sting before soothing it with his tongue, "how long I've been trying not to do this."

"Then stop trying." I arch against him, grinding down on his thigh, desperate, shameless.

He groans—low, primal—and spins me, pressing my front to the tree now, his body flush to my back. One hand grips my hip, the other wraps around my throat, thumb stroking the hollow just beneath my jaw.

Not choking. Not yet. Just holding me there. Claiming.

"This what you want?" His voice is rough silk, dangerous. "Mud on your boots, bark at your back, my cock inside you?"

"Yes," I gasp, heat flooding between my thighs. "God, yes."

He presses his face to the curve of my neck, inhaling deeply. "I've been trying to be good. To protect you from this."

I shudder as he drags his teeth along my skin. "I don't want good."

"No," he murmurs, lips brushing the shell of my ear, "you want ruin."

His hand slips beneath the hem of my shirt, calloused

fingers dragging up my bare skin, slow and possessive, until they reach the swell of my breast. He palms it roughly, thumb circling my nipple through the lace of my bra, drawing a broken sound from my throat. My hips jerk back, seeking friction, grinding against the thick line of his cock straining behind his zipper.

"Fuck, you feel like fire," he mutters, voice shaking with restraint he's fast losing. "So soft. So goddamn perfect."

He yanks down the zipper of my jeans, rough and impatient, his knuckles scraping my hips as he pushes the denim over my ass. Cold air licks over my exposed skin, but his body follows—hot and relentless. I brace against the tree, bark biting my palms, as he drags my panties down and slides his fingers between my legs.

A strangled sound tears from his chest.

"Already soaked for me. Jesus."

"Do something about it," I choke out, shivering against the assault of sensation.

He doesn't hesitate.

The sound of his fly tearing open is obscene, desperate. He lines himself up, the blunt head of his cock sliding through my slick heat, teasing my entrance. His hand fists in my hair, tugging my head back as he leans in, teeth grazing my ear.

"This is your only warning."

I don't answer. I don't need to.

He slams into me in one brutal, glorious thrust.

The breath leaves my lungs in a strangled cry, my fingers scrabbling against the tree, back arching into the searing stretch of him. He curses low and guttural, driving in deeper, hips snapping hard against my ass, again and again, pounding into me like he's making up for every second he held back.

"Mine," he growls, voice broken, lips pressed to my shoulder. "Every fucking inch of you."

"Yes." I rock back to meet him, lost in the rhythm, the ferocity, the raw need.

He thrusts harder, deeper, relentlessly, every snap of his hips a brand against my soul. I come apart fast, my orgasm crashing through me like lightning, my cry swallowed by the wind and the forest around us. My body shudders, clamps down, milking him, dragging him over the edge with me.

His shout is hoarse, his release a violent surrender as he slams deep and stills, pouring himself into me with one final, brutal thrust.

Silence falls. Only our breathing fills the space—ragged, gasping, stunned.

When we finally break for air, his forehead presses hard against mine, both of us shaking, breaths ragged.

"We need to get back to the cabin," he rasps, voice wrecked, eyes wild.

It's not a suggestion. It's a command. A promise. A threat.

I barely manage a nod before he grabs my hand, his grip unyielding, dragging me up the path with a pace that borders on brutal. Each step is a silent warning: *I'm done holding back.*

Angel's Peak

Chapter 12

The return is a blur—Caleb's hand clamps around mine, possessive, blistering with heat. His body radiates raw intent, each stride coiled with purpose. Dominance rolls off him in thick, suffocating waves, and I drink it in like oxygen. Every brush of his shoulder, every backward glance isn't just a check-in—it's a warning. A claim.

By the time the cabin appears, my pulse is a frantic staccato, my skin prickling with anticipation. Nerves strung tight and quivering

The second the door closes, he's on me.

I'm spun, slammed back against the wall, the impact stealing my breath—but it's nothing compared to the kiss. His mouth crashes onto mine with brutal hunger, all teeth and tongue, a collision of need that tastes like heat and fury and everything we've been denying. His hand fists in my hair, yanking my head back just enough to deepen the kiss, to devour me whole.

There's no gentleness—just the desperate drag of hands and the scrape of his jaw against my skin. He kisses like he's starving and I'm the last thing left.

I clutch his shirt, scrabbling to pull him closer, to feel the crushing weight of him pinning me down. He growls against my lips—low, guttural, feral—and presses his body hard to mine, hips grinding against my core until I gasp, feeling every inch of how undone he is.

"You feel that?" His voice is a snarl, hips rolling slow and punishing. "That's how much I've wanted you. How close I am to losing control."

"Then lose it," I breathe, writhing against him.

His head drops to my shoulder, jaw clenched tight. A tremor ripples through his arms, tension coiled so tight it vibrates against my skin, like a live wire ready to snap. The war inside him bleeds through every muscle, every breath, his restraint stretched thin and fraying.

A sharp inhale—then he draws back just enough to meet my gaze, eyes blazing, wild, undone.

Then his mouth crashes into mine again, and the world disappears. He doesn't kiss—he consumes. Bites down on my jaw, sucks fire into the tender spot beneath my ear until I gasp his name, breathless.

Warm knuckles brush my skin, dragging the hem of my sweater up with rough urgency. One motion—then it's gone, tossed aside, forgotten.

His gaze drops like a blow. Scorching. Possessive. Jaw locked tight like he's barely holding himself together.

"Fuck, you're perfect." He doesn't wait. Fingers hook into my bra, tugging it down with zero finesse, exposing me to the cabin's chill—and to him.

Calloused palms find me instantly—cupping, stroking— thumbs circling my nipples until my back bows with a moan, breath catching, thoughts scattering.

A growl rumbles low in his chest, vibrating against my skin as he dips his head. Lips close over one aching peak. Heat detonates—sharp, scorching—as he sucks hard, teeth scraping just enough to tear another gasp from my throat.

One hand pins my hip to the wall, the other palms my breast, rough and reverent, like he can't decide whether to worship me or wreck me.

"You drive me fucking insane," he mutters, breath ragged, voice breaking against my skin. "The way you look at me. The way you moan for me. I can't—"

The words cut off as his mouth finds mine again—harder, deeper. Teeth sink into my bottom lip before his tongue plunges in, wild and demanding. I kiss him back with everything I have, giving him everything, holding nothing back.

His hands are everywhere—shoving my jeans down, yanking my panties with them. His touch is feverish, greedy, like he's been starved, and I'm the only thing that can satisfy the hunger clawing at him. I kick off my boots, clothes tangling around my ankles, and he cages me against the wall with his body, his strength, his need.

I fumble with his buttons, but he's done waiting. A guttural sound tears from him as he shrugs off his shirt, ripping it over his head. Suddenly, it's just him—bare skin, sculpted muscle, raw power. Built for work. Built to ruin.

My hands roam over scars, ridges, and heat. I can't stop touching him. I can't get enough. He grinds against me, the thick length of him sliding through my slick heat, and I cry out—nails digging into his shoulders, back arching, body strung so tight I could snap.

There's no reprieve. No pause. Caleb doesn't give me a second to think, to breathe, to doubt. He's on me, his mouth dragging down my throat, teeth catching on the ridge of my collarbone, hands gripping my hips hard enough to bruise as he pins me tighter to the wall.

Clothes hit the floor in a blur of motion. When he steps

between my thighs, every ounce of restraint is gone. He lifts me like I weigh nothing, my legs locking around his waist, his body a wall of heat and hunger and absolute command.

The bed looms behind us, but he doesn't look. He never looks away. His eyes lock on mine like a dare, a promise, a threat. Control radiates off him—quiet, terrifying, complete.

And he walks me to the bed, all that heat and virility surging between us.

The second my back hits the mattress, he's there. On me. Over me. The crush of his weight steals my breath, and his mouth crashes onto mine like it's the only thing anchoring him to this world.

My wrists are yanked above my head, his fingers threading through mine just long enough to lock me down. The other hand slides lower—slow, deliberate—until it curls around my throat. Not choking.

Just holding.

Claiming.

A silent command that sears straight through my core.

"Before was…" His voice scrapes low, ragged, thick with something unspoken. "Rushed. Desperate." His thumb skims the hollow of my throat, feeling the frantic beat of my pulse. "I needed you too bad to be careful." His gaze traps mine—hot, unrelenting. "But this time…" He lowers his weight, his hips pressing into mine, a dark promise in every inch of contact. "This time I'm going to take my fucking time."

His hand slides over my ribcage, slow, possessive. The other stays at my throat, anchoring me.

"But don't get confused." His mouth brushes my ear, breath hot, voice darker now. "Slow doesn't mean gentle. I'm too wound up for that."

A shiver rips through me.

"You good with that?"

The question cuts through the haze. A demand wrapped in heat.

I nod, dizzy.

"Say it," he growls.

"I want everything," I gasp, arching into him. "Don't hold back."

"Good. Because I'm done pretending I can resist you." A wicked smile twists his lips.

Fumbling for protection, he barely pauses—just enough to tear the foil, roll it on—then he's back, settling between my thighs in one fluid, possessive thrust that knocks the breath from my lungs.

His rhythm is brutal from the first stroke. Hips snapping. Muscles locked. Each thrust grinds me deeper into the mattress. Every drag of his body against mine is a claim—every broken sound he rips from my throat, a victory he savors.

My wrists stay pinned, his fingers tightening around them as his other hand closes over my throat, not enough to hurt— but enough to own. My breath stutters. The world narrows to him. The pressure. The power. The heat.

"Look at me." The command cuts through the haze, voice frayed and low.

I drag my gaze up. Wild green eyes lock on mine, burning with hunger and something darker.

There's no gentleness in the way he fucks me. Just raw, unchecked need. He takes, drives, consumes—each thrust more relentless than the last, until I'm writhing, begging, broken open on a tide of pleasure too sharp to survive.

My name tears from his throat on a guttural groan as he follows me over, his body slamming into mine, shuddering with release. He collapses over me, breath hot against my neck, my name rasped like a vow against my skin.

After, he doesn't let go. He keeps me caged beneath him,

hand still wrapped around my wrist, body heavy and real, as if he's afraid I might vanish if he lets up for even a second.

And I don't want to move. I don't want to run. For the first time, I want to be exactly where I am—claimed, owned, utterly his.

The night doesn't end there. It detonates.

Caleb doesn't let me up. Not for long. Every time I think he's spent, that the storm has passed, he proves me wrong—again and again. He's a force, a relentless tide, as if years of restraint have snapped and now he can't get enough, won't ever have enough.

He takes me on my back, wrists pinned, his body heavy and commanding, driving into me until I'm breathless, hoarse from begging. He flips me, face-down, hands fisted in the sheets, his palm pressing between my shoulder blades as he fucks me from behind, rough and deep, his voice a low growl in my ear—telling me how good I feel, how he's not letting me go.

He drags me to the edge of the bed, drops to his knees, spreads my thighs wide, and buries his mouth between them, licking me until I'm shaking, sobbing, pleading for mercy he never gives.

When I come, he groans like he's starving for it, then flips me again, mouth devouring mine.

He remembers every filthy fantasy I whispered in the dark—and now he brings each one to life. Forces me to my knees, fingers tangled in my hair, guiding me as I take him deep, control absolute, praise rasping from his throat like prayer.

When I glance up, lips swollen, eyes glassy, he curses low, hauls me up, and claims me all over again.

At the window, he lifts me, pins me to the cold glass. Moonlight cuts across our skin—silver on sweat, shadow on muscle. One hand clamps around my throat, the other fists in my hair as he takes me standing, whispering every dirty promise he ever made and making good on every single one.

The wall. The floor. The bed.

Even the boulder out back—the one I teased him about once, blushing and breathless, not really thinking he'd remember. But he did. Dragged me out beneath the stars, bent me over rough stone, and made me feel his hand branding heat across my skin, his voice low and dark in my ear as I shattered for him.

He uses me everywhere, anyway he wants. Sometimes fast and punishing, driving me to the edge, making me plead for more, for mercy, for him. Other times he slows, draws it out, makes me feel every inch, every second, until I'm shaking, writhing, begging.

No matter how he takes me, he never stops reminding me who's in control. His hands own me—on my wrists, my hips, my throat. Holding me down. Pinning me open. Guiding every movement. His mouth marks me, his teeth leave proof. He wants me branded, ruined, and claimed.

And he watches—always watching. Possessive. Hungry. Reverent. Like he wants every sound I make, every tremble, every broken gasp. He wants to ruin me, and he does. Again and again, until I'm boneless, shattered, sobbing his name into the dark.

I'm raw, aching, utterly spent. He gathers me into his arms, pressing kisses to my hair, my shoulder, the hollow of my throat. His voice is rough, but there's a tenderness in it and a promise that he's not done with me yet.

I should've known better than to push.

Caleb isn't a fantasy—he's the storm that shatters fantasies.

More relentless than I ever imagined, more consuming than I can withstand, more dangerous than I was ever prepared for. He doesn't just take—he unravels. Breaks me apart with every touch, every command, until there's nothing left but need.

Even now, tangled with me in the aftermath, he's still holding back, still keeping some dark, hungry part of himself on a leash. That realization terrifies me.

Thrills me.

Some reckless, desperate part of me wants to see what happens when he finally lets it go.

"I hadn't planned this." Caleb's voice rumbles beneath my ear, low and rough, his chest rising and falling steadily beneath my cheek. "Told myself *not* to touch you. Not when you were stranded, soaked to the bone, looking for shelter. Didn't want to take advantage."

"The best laid plans…" I smile against his skin, tracing lazy circles over his heart.

"True." His arms tighten, possessive, pulling me closer so I can't mistake who I belong to. "My only regret is waiting so long to take you."

"Who knew getting caught in a storm would lead me to finding shelter with a grumpy ranger?" I tease, but my voice is soft, still raw from everything he's done to me.

"I wasn't that grumpy." A chuckle vibrates through his chest, deep and satisfied.

"You absolutely were." I prop myself up on his chest, searching his face for any sign of regret. There's none—just a relaxed openness, a dangerous contentment. "Practically snarled when you opened the door."

"In my defense, you were tracking mud everywhere." He smirks, but the words are gentle, almost indulgent.

I settle back into him, letting his warmth anchor me, the steady thump of his heart grounding me in the present.

His fingers thread through my hair, not tentative, commanding, working through the tangles with a patience that feels like ownership.

"You're not going to run from me, are you?" The question is quiet, but there's an edge to it—a challenge, a warning.

"No. Not tonight." I shake my head, breath catching.

"You tell me if you want me to stop, or if you want more." His voice is unyielding, dominant even in vulnerability.

"I'll take everything you give me. All of it. All of you." Heat floods my cheeks, my body already answering for me.

He releases my neck only to drag his thumb along my jaw, claiming me with the smallest touch. "You have no idea how much I'm still holding back."

"That should terrify me." A shiver runs through me—fear and excitement tangled, impossible to separate.

"It should." His smile turns wolfish. "But you keep pushing. You keep asking for more, and I'll bring it to you. Every dark, filthy thing you ever dreamed of. Just say the word."

"I don't know what that word is, but..." My breath stutters. "I trust you."

"You take everything I give you, so beautifully." His hand cups my jaw, tilting my face up for a slow, claiming kiss.

The words curl around me, hot and possessive, sinking straight to my core. His thumb drags along my jaw, holding me in place, gaze burning with a promise that's anything but gentle.

Caleb doesn't let me drift. He keeps me close, his dominance coiling tighter with every hour, every look. He doesn't ask what I want—he tells me, shows me, and makes me want things I never dared say out loud.

He's still holding back. Holding back because he knows all of this comes with an expiration date.

Because the day will come when I have to leave.

We lie tangled together, the aftermath heavy and sweet, his dominance still coiled around me like a second skin. Night falls as we talk—his stories, my confessions, the kind of honesty that only comes when you've been stripped bare, body and soul.

When sleep finally drags me under, I'm wrapped in his arms, his breath hot against my neck, his grip unyielding even in rest.

I feel truly wanted for the first time, which terrifies me more than any storm ever could.

Chapter 13

HEAT LINGERS IN THE STILLNESS OF THE CABIN, thick with the scent of sweat, sex, and pine. Sheets cling to damp skin, tangled around our limbs, as I surface slowly—awareness unfolding in lazy waves. Caleb's arm lies heavy across my waist, his breath steady against the back of my neck, warm and anchoring. My body aches in places I didn't know could ache—used, marked, claimed.

Last night comes rushing back in fragments: the feral hunger in his eyes, the way he broke me apart and pieced me back together with every rough, reverent touch. The way he held me after, solid and possessive, daring anything or anyone to come between us.

I shift, careful not to break the spell, just enough to see his face. In sleep, the hard lines of worry and restraint have melted away, leaving him almost boyish—unguarded, heartbreakingly beautiful.

Something fierce and unfamiliar tightens in my chest, a yearning that has nothing to do with sex and everything to do with the man beside me.

His eyes flutter open, finding mine. For a moment, confusion flickers there—then recognition, and something softer, rawer.

"Hey." His voice is rough with sleep, threaded with that dominant edge that never really leaves him.

"Hey, yourself." Suddenly, I'm shy, the reality of morning-after intimacy hitting harder than any of last night's confessions.

He doesn't let me pull away. His arm tightens, anchoring me, dragging me back into the heat of his body.

"You sleep okay?"

"Better than okay." I nuzzle closer, letting myself sink into him, grateful that awkwardness hasn't replaced what we built in the dark. "You're a surprisingly good pillow for a man who spends most of his time glowering."

"Are you saying I'm not soft?" A low chuckle rumbles through his chest, the sound vibrating into my bones.

"I'm saying you're comfortable. And I like it." I let my fingers drift over his chest, tracing the scars and muscles, staking a silent claim. "As for being soft... you're hard in all the right places."

"Damn straight, and you're not going anywhere. Not yet." His hand slides up my spine, fingers splaying wide, possessive.

The touch is gentle, but there's nothing tentative about it —he's still in control, even in this quiet moment.

The words send a shiver down my spine—part fear, part exhilaration. I'm not used to being wanted like this. I'm not used to letting myself want, either.

He rolls me beneath him in one smooth motion, his body pinning me to the mattress, eyes searching mine.

"You with me?" The question is soft, but it's not a request —it's a command, a check-in, a promise all at once.

"I'm with you." My voice is barely more than a whisper, but it's the truest thing I've ever said.

His lips find mine, and the kiss is slow, deep, a claiming

that's more about connection than conquest. There's no rush, no urgency—just the steady, inexorable heat of two people who know exactly what they want and aren't afraid to take it.

His hands explore me with a reverence that borders on worship, mapping the places that made me shatter the night before, coaxing new sounds from my lips.

When he finally joins our bodies, it's not frantic—it's profound, every movement a conversation, every thrust a confession. I cling to him, letting myself drown in the sensation, the emotion, the sense of being utterly known and utterly claimed.

After, we lie tangled together, bodies slick with sweat, hearts pounding in sync. He doesn't let me go. His hand stays heavy on my hip, thumb stroking lazy circles into my skin—a silent promise that, for now, I'm his.

The radio crackles, shattering the peace. Caleb sighs, pressing a kiss to my temple before slipping from the bed, pulling on his jeans with a grace that makes me ache.

I watch him go, drinking in the play of muscle beneath tanned skin, the way he moves with purpose even now. I stretch, cataloging the sweet ache he's left in my body, the marks of his possession hidden beneath the sheets.

When I finally emerge, clothes rumpled, hair a lost cause, Caleb stands at the radio, posture stiff, face shuttered. Something in the air has shifted.

"Copy that. Sierra Station out." He sets the handset down, turning to me with an unreadable expression.

"What is it?"

"Road crews made better progress than expected." His voice is neutral, too careful. "They think the main road will be open by tomorrow afternoon."

Relief should flood me. Instead, disappointment stabs deep, sharp, and unexpected.

"That's...good." The word tastes wrong in my mouth.

"Yeah. Good." He doesn't meet my eyes, turning away, shoulders tight.

The awkwardness we managed to outrun all morning settles between us now, thick and heavy. Caleb busies himself with coffee, his movements clipped and precise. I hover, uncertain, the distance between us suddenly more daunting than any mountain trail.

I want to reach for him. I want to ask for more. But I don't know how to bridge the gap—not when the end is suddenly so close, and I'm terrified of wanting something I might not be allowed to keep.

"Caleb." I approach slowly, uncertainty threading my voice as I rest a tentative hand on his shoulder. "Are you okay?"

He stills beneath my touch, muscles coiled tight, not leaning in but not pulling away.

"Fine." The word is clipped, too controlled. "Just thinking about everything I'll need to catch up on once the roads clear."

The deflection stings. The man who stripped me bare last night—body and soul—has retreated behind the armor of routine, as if my impending departure triggered some primal defense. I let my hand fall, the distance between us suddenly colder, sharper.

"I should check my equipment. Make sure everything's ready." I turn away, needing space to gather myself, to make sense of the ache blooming in my chest.

By the time I return, the kitchen smells of coffee and toasted bread. Caleb has set out breakfast—oatmeal with dried fruit, the last of his homemade bread drizzled with honey. He looks up as I enter, something softening in his eyes.

"Peace offering." He gestures to the steaming mug waiting for me. "Sorry about before. The news caught me off guard."

His honesty cracks the ice. I slide onto the stool beside

him, close enough that our knees brush, deliberately choosing proximity.

"Me too."

He raises an eyebrow, a silent invitation to expand and share my thoughts.

"I'm not ready to leave." The words cost more than I expect. "Which is ridiculous. I have deadlines and responsibilities. But—"

"But?" His voice is low, cautious hope flickering beneath the surface.

I meet his gaze, giving him the truth he deserves. "I'm not ready for this to end."

"There's no reason to pretend this wasn't always meant to end." He holds my gaze, jaw tight, voice rough with conviction. "We both knew what this was—went into it with our eyes wide open. No promises, no illusions."

"Right."

The word tastes like regret, sharp and unexpected. I look down, tracing the rim of my coffee mug with a finger, trying to hide the sting in my eyes.

I should agree, should feel relief at the boundaries we drew so carefully, but all I feel is the ache of wanting more. The rules we set suddenly feel like a cage.

"Yeah. No illusions." I force a small, brittle smile, but my voice comes out softer than I intend.

His hand finds mine on the table, fingers rough and sure as they lace through mine. He doesn't let go, not even as we eat —one-handed, unwilling to break this small, defiant connection.

After breakfast, he outlines his tasks for the day, which include routine maintenance, wildlife checks, and data recording. But instead of assuming I'll stay behind, he frames each as an invitation, his voice steady but his eyes searching.

"I'd like to come with you." My camera is already in my hands, the familiar weight grounding me. "If that's okay."

"More than okay." His smile is slow, transforming, banishing the last of the morning's tension.

We spend the morning together, moving through the quiet rituals of his world. At the wildlife enclosures, I watch him work—gentle with a fledgling hawk, precise as he splints a squirrel's leg, his voice low and calming as he releases a rabbit back into the wild.

I capture it all through my lens, but it's his hands, his focus, his rare, unguarded smiles that draw my attention.

"You're staring at me, not the animals." His voice is gruff, but there's a glimmer of amusement.

"You're more interesting." I lower the camera, unashamed. "The way you handle them—it's like you're speaking a language most people have forgotten."

"Just doing my job." A flush creeps up his neck, the vulnerability endearing.

"It's more than that." I snap one last photo—his profile against the green, the lock of hair falling across his brow. "You listen to them. You respect them. It's beautiful."

He clears his throat, uncomfortable but pleased. "Kim used to say the same thing."

This time, her name doesn't land between us like a wound. It's just part of his story, a ghost acknowledged and honored.

"She was right." I move closer, letting my fingers brush his arm. "You have a gift."

"Hungry?" He glances down, then gestures toward the cabin.

We return for lunch, then spend the afternoon in his office, poring over years of handwritten notes, maps, and photographs. I'm awed by the scope of his work—the patterns, the painstaking detail, the quiet passion on every page.

"This is incredible." I flip through a binder, studying seasonal photographs of the same mountain pass. "Have you ever published any of this?"

He looks genuinely surprised. "Published?"

"In journals, magazines. This is valuable. You're documenting climate change, adaptation strategies—this could help conservation efforts everywhere."

"Just keeping records." He shrugs, glancing away. "Part of the job."

"It's more than that." I turn his chair to face me, my hand firm on his shoulder. "This matters."

Something shifts in his eyes—surprise, then consideration, then a flicker of pride.

"Never thought about it that way."

"Well, start thinking." I pull out my laptop, determination settling in my bones. "I know people at National Geographic, environmental journals. They'd kill for this kind of field research—with your photos, your data, your voice."

"You really think it's worth that much?" He watches me, something fierce and tender in his gaze.

"I know it is." I nod, certain.

For a moment, we look at each other, the air thick with the possibility of what he's built, of what we could become, if only we're brave enough to claim it.

For the next hour, we work side by side, the air between us thick with unspoken things. I help Caleb organize his research, suggesting journals and conservation groups, showing him how his solitary years on the mountain could ripple out into the world.

At first, he's wary, reluctant to believe in the value of what he's done, but as we sift through his notes and photographs, I watch something shift in him—a cautious hope, a flicker of pride. The possibility that his work might matter beyond these woods, that he might matter, settles between us like a promise.

"You'd have to leave the mountain sometimes," I tease, nudging his shoulder as we compile a list of contacts. "Speak at conferences. Actually interact with people."

"Terrifying prospect." He snorts, but the smile tugging at his mouth is real.

"You'd survive." I bump his arm again, savoring the easy contact, the way his body leans into mine. "You might even like it."

"With the right company, maybe." His gaze lingers on me, heat simmering beneath the banter.

The implication hangs between us, thickening the air. I look away first, heart pounding, suddenly aware of the dangerous ground we're treading—future tense, possibilities, the kind of hope that hurts.

I'm not sure which of us is more afraid to take the next step.

As dusk settles, Caleb builds a fire in the woodstove, the flicker of flames casting gold across his skin. I chop vegetables, slice smoked trout, and the two of us move around each other in the cramped kitchen as if we've done this our entire lives.

Every brush of his hand against my back, every shared glance over the cutting board, feels charged, domestic, yes, but edged with longing, with the ache of wanting more than we're allowed.

Dinner is simple, but the intimacy of it undoes me. We eat side by side, our knees touching, as conversation drifts from the practical to the personal.

Caleb tells me about his childhood in a mountain town like this one, about learning the woods from his grandfather, about the wild freedom and loneliness of growing up half-feral.

I share stories of my own rootless life—nights spent in

tents and airports, the thrill of chasing the next shot, the ache of never belonging anywhere for long.

"Do you ever get tired of moving?" His voice is soft, vibrating against my cheek where I lean against his chest.

"Sometimes." I trace idle circles on his knee, thinking of all the empty hotel rooms, the endless blur of airport terminals. "But the next assignment is always waiting. It's what I know."

He's quiet for a moment, then his voice softens. "Is it what you want?"

The question hangs between us, heavy with everything we haven't said. I open my mouth, but before I can answer, my phone chimes—a sound so foreign after days of isolation that it startles me upright.

"Signal's back." I disentangle myself, heart racing, and grab my phone from the charger.

The screen lights up with a flood of notifications—emails, texts, voicemails, all the demands of my real life clamoring for attention.

Five missed calls from my agent, urgent. Updates on the eagle assignment. And—

"Everything okay?" Caleb's voice is careful, too neutral.

"My agent," I manage, scrolling through the messages. "National Geographic wants my eagle series for a special issue. They need confirmation immediately. It's... huge. Career-defining."

"That's good, right?" He tries for encouragement, but I hear the strain in his voice. "Your father's project, finally getting the recognition it deserves."

"It's incredible." My hands shake as I read the details. "But they need more shots. Different nesting sites, different subspecies. I'd have to be in Arizona. Immediately."

His face shutters, the warmth of moments ago replaced by a careful blankness. "You should call them back."

"Caleb—"

"It's fine." He stands, jaw tight, putting distance between us. "It's what you've been working for. You should take it."

Before I can find the words, my phone chimes again. Then again. The world outside this cabin clamors louder, demanding my attention, reminding me of everything I'm supposed to want.

"I'll give you some privacy." He grabs his jacket, his voice rough. "Need to check the perimeter before dark anyway."

The door closes behind him, and just like that, the spell breaks. I'm left alone, staring at the screen, the weight of my choices pressing down.

My life is out there, deadlines, assignments, and a career I've built from nothing. I love all of that. Worked hard for it. But all I can think about is the man who just walked out, the heat of his hands still burning on my skin, the ache of wanting more time, more of him.

The longing is unbearable, and with every second that ticks by, the end rushes closer, threatening to tear away this fragile, impossible thing we've built.

Angel's Peak

Chapter 14

Sleep eludes me long after Caleb returns from his "perimeter check"—an obvious excuse to escape the cabin and the conversation we're both avoiding. He slips into bed beside me, maintaining a careful inch of space between our bodies, close enough to feel his warmth but not touching.

The distance feels vast after days of gradually closing the gap.

Morning arrives with weak sunlight filtering through fog-shrouded windows. Caleb is already gone; his side of the bed is cold, with a note on the kitchen counter informing me that he's checking trail conditions and will be back by midday.

The terse message reads like something from our first days together, formal and impersonal.

I make coffee and toast, moving through the now-familiar kitchen with an ache of premature nostalgia. My phone, which was charged overnight, now shows no signal again. The brief connection last evening was apparently a temporary fluke rather than restored service.

The emails about the National Geographic opportunity remain partially downloaded, crucial details missing. I need more information before making any decisions. After a moment's hesitation, I turn to Caleb's desk where his satellite connection equipment sits.

"Sorry for the invasion of privacy," I mutter, powering up the system.

The connection is slow but functional, allowing my emails to fully download. The National Geographic offer unfolds in my inbox, even more impressive than the partial details suggested. They want my golden eagle photographs as the centerpiece of their endangered apex predators issue, alongside commissioned work documenting threatened eagles in Australia.

Six months on the remote western coast of Australia, capturing nesting behaviors of the endangered white-bellied sea eagle and wedge-tailed eagle. Literally, the otherside of the world from Caleb.

It's a dream assignment. The kind photographers build entire careers hoping to receive.

The deadline to accept stares back at me from the screen— 48 hours from now. If I agree, they expect me in Sydney by next week for preliminary meetings before heading to the field sites.

I sit back, my mind racing. Six months in Australia.

Half a world away from Colorado.

From Angel's Peak.

From Caleb.

The satellite connection blinks out before I can send a response, the system automatically powering down on its timer. Perhaps it's for the best—I need time to think and decide what I truly want, rather than reacting to a professional opportunity out of habit.

I busy myself cleaning the already tidy cabin, my restless energy finding an outlet in unnecessary organization. When Caleb's boots sound on the porch steps, I've swept, dusted, and rearranged his spice shelf into alphabetical order—a service he'll likely find more annoying than helpful.

The door swings open, bringing a gust of pine-scented air and Caleb's tall frame. His expression remains carefully neutral, but his eyes seek mine immediately. A flash of something unguarded crosses his features before the mask returns.

"Hey." He hangs his jacket by the door. "Roads should be clear by late afternoon. You'll be able to head out tomorrow morning."

"That's... good." The words feel hollow in my mouth. I should tell him about Australia now, and lay all the cards on the table. Instead, I ask, "How were the trails?"

"Passable." He moves to the kitchenette, maintaining distance between us. "Ridge route is completely clear. There's good visibility today."

"The eagle nesting site?"

He nods, something softening in his expression. "Perfect conditions. If you wanted one last try for your shot..."

"Really?" Hope flares despite my conflicted emotions.

"We need to leave soon to catch the right light." He glances at his watch. "I packed lunch, just in case you wanted to go."

The gesture touches me. Despite knowing I'm leaving, he's still thinking about my project and my father's legacy.

"I'd like that. Very much."

We prepare quickly, falling into the now-familiar routine of packing gear and hiking supplies. The effortlessness of our movements makes the emotional distance more painful by contrast. This could have been us, working in tandem, existing in the same rhythm.

If circumstances were different.

If I wasn't leaving.

Am I?

The hike passes in relative silence, neither of us willing to broach the topics hovering between us. Instead, Caleb points out signs of wildlife I would have missed—tracks in softened earth, marks on tree bark, subtle indications of the forest returning to normal after the storms.

The trail climbs steadily, eventually opening onto the magnificent vista I remember from our previous visit. Today, the air is exceptionally clear, and visibility extends for miles across valleys. The ridges glow emerald in the midday sun, and the cliff face where the eagle's nest stands in perfect relief against the blue sky.

"Perfect timing." Caleb gestures toward the distant nest. "Female's been hunting. She should return soon."

I unpack my camera equipment, mount the telephoto lens, and adjust the settings for the conditions. Caleb spreads a small tarp on the still-damp ground, creating a dry place to sit as we wait.

The silence between us has shifted from tense to contemplative. We're both lost in our thoughts as we scan the horizon. When his hand finds mine on the rock between us, the contact startles me—the first he's initiated since last night's revelations.

"Whatever you decide," he says quietly, eyes still on the distant peaks, "I'm glad you got stranded in my cabin."

The simple honesty steals my breath. Before I can respond, his posture straightens, and his head tilts upward. "Three o'clock. Coming in from the south."

I follow his gaze, camera raised instinctively. Through the telephoto lens, I spot it—the magnificent golden eagle soaring on thermal currents, its wings extended in a majestic span, sunlight burnishing its feathers to a living bronze. It circles slowly, riding invisible air currents with effortless grace.

"It's beautiful," I whisper, tracking the bird's movement through my viewfinder.

"She's heading for the nest." Caleb's voice remains low,

mindful of carrying sound despite our distance. "Probably bringing food for the mate."

Sure enough, the eagle banks toward the cliff face, something clutched in her mighty talons. I adjust focus, finger hovering over the shutter release, waiting for the perfect moment.

The eagle approaches the nest with wings extended for landing, sunlight catching every detail of its magnificent plumage, the power in its form, the intensity of its focus. Time seems to slow as I find the composition I've been seeking for days—no, the one my father sought for years.

The essence of this apex predator captured in a single, perfect frame.

I press the shutter, and the camera's rapid fire captures a sequence of her landing. I've got it—the shot my father never managed to get, the one that eluded him through decades of patient watching.

"Got it?" Caleb asks, watching my face rather than the eagle.

"Yes." Emotion thickens my voice. "The perfect shot. Exactly what Dad was looking for all those years."

His hand squeezes mine, understanding the significance without need for explanation. "He'd be proud."

I lower the camera, and unexpected tears blur my vision. "Project complete." The words emerge bittersweet, accomplishment tangled with the realization that my purpose for being in Angel's Peak is fulfilled.

We sit in silence, watching the eagles interact at the distant nest, sharing food and performing the small rituals of mated pairs. The domesticity of these fierce predators strikes me with unexpected poignancy—they mate for life. Return to the same nest year after year, maintaining bonds that transcend seasons.

"You're very quiet." Caleb's observation breaks my reverie.

"Just thinking." I review the shots on my camera's

display, confirming what I already know—I have exactly what I need, what my father wanted. "Mission accomplished, I guess."

"You don't sound happy about it."

"It's complicated." I meet his eyes, finding concern there alongside wariness.

"Because of the National Geographic assignment?"

"You knew?" His directness catches me off guard.

"I saw the email flash on your phone when I checked the satellite system this morning. Just the subject line. I wasn't snooping. Australia, right?"

Heat rises to my cheeks. "I was going to tell you. I just... needed to process it first."

"Six months is a significant commitment." His expression remains carefully neutral. "Good opportunity."

"It's more than good. It's career-defining." I set the camera aside, turning to face him. "Eagles in Australia—continuing exactly the kind of work my father did, but for the most prestigious nature publication in the world. Officially on assignment for National Geographic. It's everything I've hoped for. More than I ever thought I'd..."

"It sounds perfect for you." His voice holds genuine approval, not the bitterness I half-expected. "When do you leave?"

"Next week. If I accept." I look down at our still-joined hands, his larger one enveloping mine on the sun-warmed stone. "I haven't given them an answer yet."

"What's holding you back?" The question pierces straight to the heart of my conflict.

"You know what's holding me back." I meet his eyes, refusing to pretend we don't both understand what's developed between us.

"Harper... we've known each other for a matter of days." A faint line appears between his brows.

"I'm aware of the timeline." Defensive edges creep into my voice. "That doesn't make it less real."

His hand stills, tension creeping into the space between us. "I'm not saying it's not real. I'm saying it's fast. Intense circumstances... they can blur the lines. Make everything feel sharper, deeper."

"You make it sound so clinical. Is that how you feel? Everything that's happened between us is... situational?" The suggestion stings more than it should, pride wounded alongside something deeper.

"No. That's not what I mean." He exhales, slow and heavy. "What we've shared—it matters. But I need to be sure it's more than just the storm talking. More than adrenaline and isolation and needing someone to hold on to."

He runs a hand through his hair, frustration evident in the gesture. "We have to be realistic. You live on planes and in hotels, following stories around the world. I'm here, committed to this mountain and this forest."

"And those facts are suddenly revelations?" I stand, needing physical movement to relieve the tension in my chest. "You knew who I was, what I do, when you kissed me. When you took me to your bed."

"And you knew I would stay." His voice remains steady despite the flash of emotion in his eyes. "That I built a life here for reasons that haven't changed."

"So what was this?" I gesture between us, anger rising to cover hurt. "A convenient distraction during bad weather? Cabin fever with benefits?"

"That's not fair." He stands, too, his height advantage forcing me to tilt my head to maintain eye contact. "What happened between us is real, but real doesn't automatically mean lasting."

The truth in his words cuts deeper than accusations would have.

"So that's it? Thanks for the memories, have a nice life in Australia?"

"That's not what I'm saying." Frustration edges his tone for the first time. "I'm saying we need to be practical about this. You have an incredible opportunity that aligns perfectly with your life's work. Your father's legacy. I'm not going to stand in the way of that. It's not the kind of man I am."

"And what if I'm reconsidering what my life's work looks like?" The question emerges before I've fully formed the thought.

"Are you?" His gaze sharpens, searching my face. "Is that what you were thinking *before* you knocked on my door? Or are you caught up in the romance of finding connection in an unexpected place?"

The question hits uncomfortably close to my unexamined feelings.

"That's not fair."

"Life rarely is." His expression softens slightly. "I care about you. More than I ever expected to, more than I wanted to, if I'm being completely honest. But I won't let you turn down the kind of opportunity you've worked your entire career to earn."

"That's not your decision to make." Indignation rises, familiar and comforting compared to the complicated emotions beneath it.

"No, it's yours." He steps closer, voice gentling. "And you should make it without the pressure of whatever this is between us. Without romantic notions clouding your professional judgment."

"You think that's what's happening?" I wrap arms around myself, suddenly cold despite the warm sunshine. "That I'm some lovesick girl ready to throw away my career for a man I just met?"

"I think you're conflicted. I think what's happened

between us has been intense and unexpected for both of us." His hands lift, hover like they want to reach for me, then fall uselessly to his sides.

"And you're a complicating factor." My voice comes out flatter than I intend, the quiet hurt behind it masked by pride.

His jaw tightens. "We both are."

He looks past me, out toward the horizon, but I feel the shift—like I'm already slipping out of reach. "This place, the storm... it created a bubble. A space where everything felt heightened. Real. And it is. But that doesn't mean it can survive outside of it."

"You're saying it's not real."

"No." He turns back to me, eyes shadowed with something too deep for words. "I'm saying it *feels* real, because it *is* *real*. But that doesn't mean it's meant to last beyond this."

The ache in my chest cracks wider.

"I would never ask you to give up your dreams," he says softly, "not for me. Not for something that might not survive once we're back in the world where deadlines and decisions and distance are real."

"So this is you... what? Letting me go before I even decide to stay?"

He shakes his head, grief buried behind quiet resolve. "This is me loving you enough not to let what we have become something you'll regret."

My breath catches.

Loving me.

He said it. Not in a grand declaration or sweeping vow, but quietly. Unflinchingly. As if it's always been true.

And that's what undoes me.

Not the part where he's trying to protect my future.

Not the part where he's already preparing for goodbye.

But the part where he's doing it out of love.

Because Caleb isn't walking away from me.

He's walking away *for* me.

"We should head back. You'll want to be packed and ready when the roads clear."

The hike down passes in strained silence, the camaraderie of earlier replaced by physical and emotional distance. We move efficiently, speaking only when necessary about trail conditions or approaching weather. The comfortable vibe between us is replaced by awkward tension and distance.

When the cabin finally comes into view, that tension has crystallized into something brittle and painful.

Caleb stops at the forest's edge, gesturing toward the structure that was a prison, then a sanctuary, and now simply a temporary accommodation.

"I need to check the eastern trail before dark. Radio, if you need anything."

The transparent excuse to avoid further conversation should irritate me. Instead, it just aches.

"Caleb—"

"It's better this way." His eyes meet mine briefly before sliding away. "Cleaner."

He's gone before I can respond, disappearing into the forest with the efficiency of someone who belongs there far more than I ever could.

I watch until his form vanishes among the trees, then continue to the cabin that suddenly feels emptier than when I first arrived.

Inside, I move mechanically through packing, gathering scattered belongings from corners where they've migrated during my stay. Each item collected feels like dismantling evidence of my presence here, erasing traces of days that already seem dreamlike in their intensity.

He's giving me the perfect out—a way to leave without complications. It's exactly what the old Harper would want.

So why does it feel so wrong?

Angel's Peak

Chapter 15

Evening descends with the finality of an executioner's axe.

Shadows bleed long and dark across the cabin floor as I fold the last of my clothes into my backpack. Each item carries a weight. Each zipper tug a *goodbye* I don't want to say out loud. The room smells like pine and ash and him. Like the silence that's settled thick between us.

The radio crackles on Caleb's desk, a harsh, static-laced sound that slices through the stillness like a warning shot.

"Sierra Station, this is Dispatch. Do you copy?"

I freeze. My heart clenches. There it is. The thing we've both been pretending wouldn't come.

Caleb, silent since returning an hour ago, looks up from the notes he's been pretending to organize. His jaw flexes, and then he moves to the radio, his voice low and steady. Controlled.

"Sierra Station. Go ahead, Dispatch."

"Roads are officially cleared to Blue Spruce Campground. Rangers will be passing your location at 0800 tomorrow for

supply delivery. Can arrange transport for your visitor if needed."

His eyes meet mine across the room. The look holds me still. Like a hand wrapped tight around my ribs.

"Copy that. She'll be ready. Sierra Station out."

He sets the handset down with a kind of care that's louder than a slam. I can't breathe around the pressure in my chest.

"So. Tomorrow morning," he says.

"Tomorrow morning," I echo, fingers worrying the zipper of my bag like it's something I can control. "Sounds like my eviction notice is official."

The joke dies before it lands. Caleb doesn't laugh. Doesn't even smirk. He turns his back, rifling through papers that definitely don't need rifling.

"Need anything for the trip back? Water, snacks?"

"I'm good." I buckle my pack like I'm bracing for battle. "Though I should probably call my agent once I have reliable service. The deadline for the Australia position—"

"Right." He cuts me off. No hesitation. No softness. "You must be eager to get back to civilization. Real showers, decent coffee."

"The coffee here isn't half bad." I force a smile that feels more like a fracture.

A pause.

"And the company has been... unexpected."

His shoulders tense, broad and unmoving beneath his flannel, but when he turns, something in his expression cracks open. Just a little.

"Harper—"

The radio interrupts again. A mercy or a curse, I'm not sure. I back away, retreating to the window seat where twilight presses up against the glass. Caleb's voice turns official again as he speaks to Dispatch, but I barely register the words.

Outside, the forest gives way to darkness. Every tree swallowed by shadow. And with the night comes the cold, creeping in beneath the seams of the cabin—and beneath my skin.

It's the slow, inevitable unraveling of something that never got a chance to begin.

When the radio finally goes quiet, Caleb moves to the kitchenette, his silhouette tall and backlit in the amber glow of a single lamp.

"Hungry?"

"Not really."

Not for food. Not when I'm already choking on goodbye.

"Should eat something anyway."

He pulls together a quiet meal—bread, cheese, smoked trout. The last of what we have. We sit across from each other, knees almost touching under the narrow table. Every motion is deliberate. Every glance held too long, or not at all.

Passing the water pitcher. Reaching for the salt. My fingers brush his, and the contact lingers longer than it should. Static, heat, tension. And then nothing. We keep going like it didn't happen.

Afterward, I help with the dishes. Close quarters. Barely enough room to turn without touching. But we don't. Somehow, we manage not to.

The silence between us now feels like its own kind of storm.

"I should double-check my gear," I say, just to break it. Just to run.

But when I look up, Caleb's already watching me. And that look—raw, unreadable, carved from whatever we've been trying not to say—stops me cold.

"Harper."

My name lands like an anchor, stopping me halfway to the bedroom. I turn. Caleb stands braced against the counter, arms tense and knuckles white, gripping the edge like it's the only thing keeping him from coming after me.

"I don't want our last night to be like this."

His voice is low. Raw. Honest in a way that slices clean through every wall I've managed to hold in place.

"I don't either." Something inside me cracks.

He pushes away from the counter. Slow. Deliberate. Like every step costs him something. He closes half the space between us, enough to feel the gravity between our bodies begin to pull.

"I meant what I said earlier. About your opportunity. About not complicating your decision." His voice hitches just slightly. "But that doesn't mean I want you to leave with this heaviness between us."

"What do you suggest?" My throat tightens.

"Just us. Right now. Before real life reclaims us both." His eyes hold mine—steady, unwavering. But there's something unspoken beneath the surface. Vulnerability threaded through determination.

It shouldn't be enough.

The offer is too clean. Too easy. But it's everything. One last perfect ache. One more memory carved into the marrow of who we are.

Pride says *walk away*.

Fear says *don't get hurt again*.

But something deeper, quieter, and more desperate recognizes this for what it is. It's the only kind of truth either of us can give.

"I'd like that," I whisper, and cross the final distance between us until there's nothing left but heat and breath and unspoken want.

His hand rises to my face, rough palm cupping my cheek like I'm something sacred. His thumb brushes the corner of my mouth.

But his eyes—God, his eyes—they say *everything*.

When his mouth finds mine, it's not frantic or rushed. It's slow. Soul-deep. A kiss that tastes like goodbye and reverence, all tangled together. My arms wind around his neck. His wrap around my waist. He pulls me in like he's memorizing the shape of missing me.

Time bends. Folds. Each sensation sharper because we both know what's coming. The rasp of his stubble against my jaw. The scent of him—smoke and pine and heat. The way his hands grip tight, then gentler, then tight again, like he can't decide between holding on and letting go.

We move through the cabin in pieces. My sweater caught on the back of a chair. His flannel shirt landing near the woodstove. Every layer discarded like a truth we're no longer afraid to show.

By the time we reach the bed, we're skin to skin. Warmth against warmth. His heartbeat a steady drum beneath my palm.

This time there's no rush. No storm outside or urgency inside. Just this.

Him.

Me.

The breath between kisses. The way his hands map my body like he's learning it, memorizing it. I trace every scar. Every line. Every place I'll miss too much.

"You're beautiful," he says, voice thick, barely holding together.

I can't answer. The lump in my throat swells too high. So I pull him down instead, and show him everything I can't speak.

This isn't just sex. It's surrender. Worship. It's grief in the shape of intimacy.

When he moves inside me, it feels like coming home to something I never believed I could deserve. His name breaks from my lips in a whisper, and I swear I feel him tremble.

We don't make love.

We say goodbye with every touch. Every breath. Every trembling heartbeat that dares to hope the morning won't come.

Every motion is deliberate. Every breath shared. His eyes never leave mine, anchoring me in something deeper than sensation. I ride the edge, breath catching, heart racing, and when the tension finally breaks, it's his name that tears from me—a broken whisper made of want and wonder.

He follows with a shudder against my skin, his face buried in the crook of my neck. My name leaves his lips like a confession, like a prayer. I wrap my arms around him and hold tight, not knowing how to let go.

Afterward, we lie tangled in the dark. My head rests on his chest, the steady beat of his heart grounding me. His fingers trace aimless, featherlight shapes along my spine—circles, lines, something that feels like a memory in the making.

The silence has changed. No longer tense or unfinished. Now it's full. Quiet, sacred.

Outside, the wind threads through the pine boughs, soft and constant. Nature's lullaby, wrapping around the hush between us.

"I didn't plan for this." His voice rumbles beneath my ear, a sound I feel more than hear. It vibrates through his chest, into my bones.

"No one plans for a bedraggled photographer to get stranded on their doorstep in a thunderstorm." I try to make it light. But my voice catches on the truth I'm not quite ready to say. "But I don't regret it. Nor do I regret feeling this way."

I shift, rising just enough to see his face. Moonlight kisses the sharp lines of his jaw, softens the raw honesty in his eyes.

"What way?"

His gaze holds mine. No deflection. No escape.

"Like I've found something I didn't know I was missing."

The words hit with the force of a heartbeat skipping a beat.

"Caleb—"

"I know. No promises. No expectations." His thumb brushes the curve of my bottom lip, so gently that it makes my throat ache. "But I need you to know—this wasn't casual for me. It never was."

"For me, either." The truth slips free without resistance. It feels right here, in the dark, in the warmth of him. "I don't want to lose this."

He searches my face. Not pushing. Just present.

"What do you want?"

The question lingers in the air, heavy and full of dangerous hope.

"I don't know." The words tremble, real, and rough. "Everything's happening so fast. The National Geographic offer, us... I haven't had time to think clearly."

"I understand." And somehow, I believe him. There's no edge in his voice, no expectation—just steady, unwavering patience.

"But I've never felt this way before." I flatten my palm against his chest, feel the warmth of him, the rhythm I've already memorized. "Not with anyone."

"Even with such a short timeline?" A flicker of his earlier wariness returns, softened now by something warmer. Something that wants to believe.

"Maybe because of it." I lower myself back to him, cheek to his chest, letting the steady thrum of his heartbeat pull me under. "No time for masks or games. Just... us. Stripped bare."

His fingers start moving again. Slow. Soothing.

"Kim and I dated for two years before getting engaged. Thought we had it all figured out." Her name doesn't wound him anymore. It drifts between us like a leaf in the current.

"But looking back... I'm not sure we ever had the kind of honesty that happened between us this week."

"Different circumstances," I murmur.

"Maybe." His hand stills on my lower back. A breath stretches between us. "Or maybe *this* is something else entirely."

We fall silent again, each lost in private thoughts about possibilities and limitations, desires and realities.

His breathing steadies. The heat of his body wraps around me like a cocoon, anchoring me to this impossible moment. I try to memorize it all—his scent, the way his chest rises and falls beneath my cheek, the lazy drag of his fingers along my spine.

Sleep creeps in at the edges, soft and insistent.

"I don't want you to give up your dream." His voice is a low murmur, threading through the haze of almost-sleep. "That National Geographic assignment—it's everything you've worked for."

"I know." My reply is drowsy, slurred by exhaustion and the ache of goodbye.

He's quiet for a beat.

"But I don't want to lose you before I've properly found you either."

That—*that*—breaks something open inside me. The vulnerability in it reaches past my slipping consciousness. I want to answer, to offer him something true, something brave —but sleep pulls me under before I can shape the words.

The last thing I feel is his arms tightening around me. Holding on. Just a little longer.

But morning comes too soon.

Pale light filters through the window, illuminating the tangle of sheets and limbs. I wake slowly, reluctantly, letting awareness wash over me in slow, aching waves.

Caleb breathes steadily beside me, one arm draped across

my waist, his body warm where it presses into mine. I lie still, letting myself pretend—just for a heartbeat—that this is normal. That we have more mornings like this ahead.

But reality seeps in. The sound of an approaching engine, too steady to be wind or wildlife. A Forest Service vehicle, right on schedule.

Time's up.

Caleb stirs. His arm tightens around me for one last, instinctive second before he exhales and pulls away.

"Morning." His voice is sleep-rough, deep, and intimate.

"Morning." I don't move. Not yet. I want to hold on to these last seconds where we're still an *us*.

We both know what's coming. Neither of us says it.

The sound of the engine grows louder, breaking the fragile stillness. Caleb rolls out of bed and runs a hand through his hair, the movement so familiar now it hurts to watch.

"That'll be your ride."

I nod, my throat too tight to speak.

We dress in silence, the domesticity suddenly sharp-edged. My sweater smells like woodsmoke. His flannel ends up draped over the chair where I left it last night.

Every motion feels like a goodbye.

I check my gear, pack my bag, and tuck my camera away like it's the only piece of this place I can take with me. My heart feels heavier than my pack.

Outside, the engine cuts off. Doors slam. Voices call his name. He heads toward the door, pausing with one hand on the knob.

"Ready?"

I nod. It's a lie.

Two rangers wait outside, smiling. A woman with a short buzz cut. A tall man with a salt-and-pepper beard. Their warmth feels almost cruel.

"You must be the stranded photographer. Name's Hamilton." The woman extends her hand. "Sounds like you've had quite the adventure."

"Harper Wells." I force a smile, brittle at the edges. "Adventure's one word for it."

"Marty Shore," the older man introduces himself. "We should be able to get you back to recover your gear. Flooding was pretty severe, but the parking lot remained dry. Your car is good. Can't say the same about the rest of your gear."

"Well, that's one good thing. Gear is replaceable. The rental would've been a pain to deal with if it had been destroyed."

"You're not wrong about that." Hamilton loads my gear into their vehicle.

Caleb helps, his expression neutral, his movements efficient. When his eyes meet mine, the weight of everything unsaid presses down like snowfall.

When it's done, the rangers give us a few minutes under the guise of checking tire pressure. Caleb and I stand before the cabin. The place that held a storm—and something more.

"So."

"So."

We mirror each other. Guarded. Unsure.

"Safe travels," he says. Too formal. Too distant.

"Thanks for the shelter. And everything else."

He nods. Looks away. I wait, praying for something more.

When he looks back, emotion flickers across his face. But the mask returns too fast.

"You should go. Don't want to hold up the rangers."

"Right."

I turn. Start walking.

Behind me—

"Harper."

I stop. Don't turn. Can't.

"I meant what I said last night. All of it."

Tears sting. I nod. Just once. Then I climb into the truck. Seatbelt clicks. The engine rumbles.

I look back.

He stands in front of the cabin, still as stone. Watching until the trees swallow the road between us.

I've spent my life leaving places behind, but leaving him feels like I'm making the worst mistake of my life.

Angel's Peak

Chapter 16

The forest service truck jostles along the recently cleared road, each turn taking me further from the cabin. Further from Caleb.

Hamilton chatters about the storm damage, pointing out places where landslides nearly took out entire sections of the route. I respond with appropriate noises of interest, but my mind remains back at the cabin, replaying our goodbye that wasn't really a goodbye at all.

"You okay back there?" Marty catches my eye in the rearview mirror. "Looking a little green. Road's still rough in spots."

"I'm fine." I force a smile that doesn't reach my eyes. "Just... processing the last week."

"Must've been intense." Hamilton twists in her seat to face me. "Stuck with the mountain hermit for all that time."

"Mountain hermit?" The description doesn't fit the complex man I've come to know.

"That's what some of the team calls Donovan." She grins, apparently unaware of the complicated emotions churning through me. "Nice guy, don't get me wrong, but he keeps to himself. Been that way since he transferred here after..." She trails off, clearly unsure how much I know about Caleb's past.

"After the Carson Ridge fire," I finish for her, surprising her with my knowledge. "He told me about it."

Marty's eyebrows rise, visible in the mirror. "He did? Wow. Took me two years of working with him before he mentioned Kim's name."

The casual revelation that Caleb shared something with me he rarely discusses with colleagues adds another layer to the ache spreading through my chest.

I turn to the window, watching the trees flash by, each one taking me closer to my regular life and further from the unexpected detour that's shaken its foundation.

"There's your campsite coming up." Hamilton points ahead where blue tents are visible through the trees. "Blue Spruce Campground. All your stuff they could save should still be there—rangers secured the sites during evacuation."

My rental car sits where I left it, seemingly ages ago though barely a week has passed. The sight of it—this connection to my normal life—should bring relief. Instead, it feels like a stranger's vehicle, belonging to a version of myself I'm no longer certain exists.

Marty helps unload my gear, setting it beside my car while Hamilton checks that the campsite has been properly maintained in my absence. I go through the motions of thanking them, assuring them I'm fine to continue alone, all while feeling increasingly hollow inside.

As they prepare to leave, Hamilton hands me a card. "If you're ever back in Angel's Peak, give us a call. Would love to see those eagle shots when they're published."

"I will." I tuck the card into my pocket, knowing I'll keep it even as I doubt I'll make that call. Returning would be too painful if...

I shake off the thought, waving as they drive away before

turning to my campsite and rental car. First things first—assess the damage, reorganize, and figure out next steps. The routine of packing proper equipment helps ground me, giving purpose to movements that might otherwise falter under emotional weight.

My phone vibrates in my pocket, the signal fully restored now that I'm back in range of civilization. Messages flood in, most prominently from my agent: "CALL IMMEDIATELY re: Nat Geo. Deadline tomorrow!"

Reality crashes back, demanding decisions I've momentarily pushed aside in the emotional fog of leaving Caleb. The Australia assignment—six months documenting endangered eagles on the other side of the world. A career-defining opportunity that perfectly aligns with my father's legacy. The very definition of perfect timing.

So why does it feel so wrong?

I start the car, needing to reach the motel in Angel's Peak where I can shower properly and sort through my thoughts. As I navigate the winding forest road, memories of the past week play through my mind—Caleb's reluctant hospitality that first stormy night, our gradual building of trust, and the surprising depth of connection that developed in such a short time.

And the sex. Especially the night—and day—when Caleb unleashed the darkness inside of him, treating me to some of the best sex I've ever had.

The town appears through the trees, a picturesque mountain community of wooden buildings and hanging flower baskets. I check into Mable's Guest House, a rustic but clean B&B with reliable Wi-Fi—my lifeline back to my regular existence.

After the longest shower of my life, washing away a week of minimal bathing with limited water, I sit on the edge of the bed, staring at my phone.

The National Geographic number glows on the screen, my thumb hovering over the call button.

One call and I commit to six months in Australia.

One call and I leave Angel's Peak behind.

One call, and I leave Caleb firmly in the past.

What's stopping me? This is exactly the kind of opportunity I've worked my entire career to earn.

Instead of making the call, I open my camera and scroll through the images from the past week. The majestic eagle in perfect flight. The fox family playing near their den. The mountain vistas in shifting weather.

And Caleb.

Caleb kneeling beside injured wildlife, tending them with gentle hands.

Caleb explaining forest conservation with rare animation.

Caleb gazing at the mountains with quiet reverence for the wilderness he protects.

I stop at an image captured without his knowledge—his profile against the setting sun as he explained the eagle's nesting habits. Something in his expression, the rare contentment visible in the softened lines of his face, pierces me anew.

My phone rings, startling me from reverie. My agent's name flashes on the screen.

"Harper! Finally!" David's voice bursts through the speaker. "Where have you been? I've been trying to reach you for days!"

"Stranded in a storm. No signal." I clear my throat, trying to sound more professional than I feel. "I got your messages about National Geographic."

"Are you sitting down? Six months in Australia, full expenses, exclusive rights to your eagle series, and prime placement in their endangered predators issue. It's the break we've been waiting for."

"I know." My voice sounds distant. "It's an incredible opportunity."

"Incredible? It's career-defining. They need your answer by tomorrow. The paperwork is in your email—just sign and return, and you're booked on a flight to Sydney next week."

"Next week," I repeat, the timeline suddenly very real.

"Is there a problem?" David's tone shifts from excitement to concern. "Harper? You sound off."

"No problem." I force enthusiasm I don't feel. "Just processing. It's a big commitment."

"Six months flies by in this business. You'll be back before you know it, with a major international credit to your name and connections that will set you up for life."

"Right." I stare at Caleb's image on my camera screen. "Let me review the paperwork. I'll call you in the morning with my decision."

"Decision? Harper, there's nothing to decide. This is a yes, obviously." Confusion colors his voice. "What's going on?"

"Nothing. I just need to... think." I end the call before he can protest further, dropping the phone onto the bed beside me.

Hours later, I've reviewed the contract multiple times without absorbing the details. My thoughts remain entangled, torn between professional opportunities and personal connections.

The rational choice is clear—take the assignment, advance my career, continue the nomadic existence that has defined my adult life.

Why does the thought of leaving Angel's Peak—leaving Caleb—feel like tearing out something essential?

CHAPTER 17

Unable to remain confined in the motel room with my circling thoughts, I grab my keys and head out.

The evening air carries the crisp scent of pine and approaching autumn. The streets are quiet as the small town prepares for the night. I find myself driving back toward the forest and the trailhead leading to Caleb's cabin.

I won't go all the way, I tell myself. Just need to clear my head in the forest air.

The parking area at the trailhead sits empty as darkness falls. I leave my car, taking only my camera out of habit, and step onto the now-familiar path. The forest welcomes me with rustling leaves and the occasional call of a night bird, the trail visible in the light of a nearly full moon.

I walk without purpose, letting my feet follow remembered routes while my mind grapples with the choice before me. The career I've built versus the connection I've found. The known path versus the uncertain one.

A sound stops me—mechanical, out of place in the natural setting. I freeze, listening. There it comes again—metal on metal, followed by low voices. Instinct sends me off the main trail, moving quietly through underbrush toward the source.

The moon provides just enough light to navigate by as I approach a small clearing. Through the trees, I make out two figures working by the light of their headlamps, setting something on the ground before moving a few yards away to repeat the process.

Traps. They're setting traps.

My photographer's instincts kick in, camera rising to capture evidence in the low light. The telephoto lens brings the scene into sharp focus—two men placing what appear to be large steel-jaw traps, illegal in most states and certainly in a protected forest.

The angle of their headlamps catches distinctive markings on the traps—custom modifications I recognize from a conservation piece I shot last year on wildlife trafficking. These aren't random poachers; they're part of an organized operation targeting specific animals.

The placement near the base of the ridge, where Caleb showed me the nesting sites, can't be a coincidence.

They're after talons and feathers, which are valuable on the black market.

I document their activities silently, cold anger replacing my earlier emotional turmoil. When they move deeper into the forest, I retreat carefully, heading not for my car but for the cabin. Caleb needs to see this immediately.

The hike to the ranger station takes longer in the darkness, but determination drives me forward. When the cabin finally appears through the trees, windows glowing with warm light, relief washes through me. I rush the final yards, taking the porch steps two at a time before pounding on the door.

It swings open almost immediately, revealing Caleb in worn jeans and a faded t-shirt, hair damp as if from a recent shower. His expression transforms from confusion to shock as he registers my presence.

"Harper? What—"

"Poachers." I push past him into the cabin, already retrieving my camera to show him the evidence. "Setting eagle traps on the north ridge. I caught them in the act."

His professional training takes over instantly, and personal complications are set aside in the face of a threat to his forest. He examines my photos, asking questions about locations and timing while gathering equipment.

"How many men?"

"Two that I saw. They had a vehicle parked off Forest Road 22, just past the creek crossing."

He nods, reaching for his radio to call it in. Within minutes, he's coordinated with other rangers, establishing a containment plan to catch the poachers before they can retrieve their traps or escape the area.

"I need to go before they finish setting their line." He shrugs into his jacket, checking his gear with efficient movements. "You should stay here. They could be dangerous."

"Not happening." I match his preparations, already heading for the door. "I can identify exactly where they were working. And we both know I move quietly in the forest."

"Stay behind me. Do exactly as I say."

His words cut through the space between us—low, firm, unyielding. That voice. That tone. It hits like a lightning strike straight to the center of me.

"Yes, sir!" I snap a salute for some stupid reason, trying to inject humor into the moment.

Instead, my body reacts before my brain can catch up—shoulders pulling back, breath hitching, heat blooming low and hot. It's not fear that curls inside me. It's memory.

Hunger.

The ghost of the man who owned every inch of my body with a single command.

That wasn't how it was the last time. The last time, it was tender. Careful. Loving. But this side of Caleb is the part I ache for and haven't dared ask to return.

If I were staying, things would be different.

Our eyes lock. A breath. A tremble.

And something shifts in him.

His gaze dips—subtle, fast. The flicker of his eyes over my face, the way his jaw tics. He feels it. Registers it. The pulse of heat he just summoned without meaning to.

He swallows hard, breath tight as he nods, tone clipped, professional, but his voice cracks around the edges of restraint.

"Don't do that, Harper."

"Do what?" I give a half-smile—weak, brittle. A reflex against the ache twisting inside me.

"You know exactly what I mean." He doesn't smile back. Not really. Just a flicker in his eyes before he shuts it all down, the moment locked away behind the rigid lines of control.

He turns. Takes the lead. Not in the way I crave—not as the man who took control with a growl and made me come undone with nothing but his dominance and a well-placed command—but as a Ranger on a mission to catch poachers.

And I follow, pulse pounding, still chasing the ghost of the command that lit me up from the inside.

We move through the moonlit forest, communication reduced to hand signals and occasional whispered directions. Despite the circumstances, I'm struck by our seamless coordination, the way we anticipate each other's movements without needing to discuss them.

We locate the first trap exactly where I saw the men place it. Caleb disarms it, explaining in whispers that they'll rearm it later with tracking devices after documenting its location. We continue along the poachers' route, finding and disarming another six traps strategically placed to catch eagles coming down to hunt at dawn.

"They know the patterns." Anger edges Caleb's whisper as he examines a particularly vicious mechanism. "These are professionals."

"Targeting golden eagles specifically." I photograph each trap in place before he disarms it. "The market for ceremonial feathers is booming overseas. A single tail feather can bring hundreds of dollars."

His eyebrow raises slightly. "You know a lot about wildlife trafficking."

"Did a series on it last year. These trap modifications—" I point to distinctive markings, "—match ones used by a ring operating out of Denver."

The respect in his eyes warms me, as if his praise is the only thing that matters. We continue our careful documentation, working in tandem until all the traps we can find are neutralized. By the time we finish, other rangers have radioed confirmation that they've located the poachers' vehicle and established surveillance.

"They'll catch them when they return to check the traps." Caleb secures the last piece of evidence in his pack. "Your photographs will be crucial for prosecution."

We hike back toward the cabin in the predawn darkness, adrenaline gradually ebbing to leave exhaustion in its wake. Reality returns as the structure comes into view—I should be miles away by now, heading toward the airport and Australia.

"I missed my checkout at the motel." The realization comes abruptly as moonlight silvers the cabin roof. "And I'm supposed to call my agent with my decision about Australia in..." I check my watch, "...three hours."

Caleb stops at the edge of the clearing, turning to face me. In the pale moonlight, his expression holds none of yesterday's careful guardedness, replaced by something raw and honest.

"What are you going to tell him?"

The question hangs between us, fraught with possibilities. I take a deep breath, finally giving voice to the truth I've been circling for days.

"I don't want to go." The admission feels simultaneously terrifying and liberating. "I should want to. It's everything I've worked for. But..."

"But?" His voice holds careful neutrality, giving me space to find my answer.

"But I'm not sure if I want to keep moving, or if I've just been afraid to stay still." The insight emerges fully formed, surprising even me with its clarity. "After watching my mom fall apart when Dad left, I swore I'd never be that vulnerable. Never need anyone or any place enough to break if I lost it."

"So you keep moving. Never putting down roots." Understanding dawns in his eyes.

"Tonight, working with you to protect these eagles, this place..." I gesture toward the forest around us. "It felt right in a way my work hasn't for a long time. Not just capturing beauty, but protecting it. Being part of something lasting."

"You could do that anywhere." Though his words suggest distance, his tone holds something like hope. "Including Australia."

"I could." I step closer, heart pounding with what I'm considering. "But I'm not sure I want to."

"What do you want, Harper?"

The question emerges rough, like it scrapes up from somewhere deep, ragged with emotion barely contained.

"I don't know," I say, breath hitching. "But I *do* know I don't want to run away from this. Not from you. Not from whatever this is between us."

He inhales sharply, like the air's suddenly too thick. His control frays at the edges.

"And Australia?"

"It can wait." The words come out without hesitation, surprising even me with their clarity. "There will still be assignments in six months. A year. But this feels like something I'd regret not exploring."

His eyes search mine. A storm gathering.

"Why would you give up your dreams?"

My voice softens, honesty trembling beneath it. "Because I keep hoping you'll tell me to stay."

"Harper... I won't do that." He stiffens. Shakes his head.

"What if I said I wanted you to *make* me stay?"

"That's not my place." His mouth parts, shocked stillness stretching between us. "What little time we've spent together doesn't give me that right."

"What if I want it to?" The words spill out, raw and quiet. "What if what we started—what we *touched*—is more than one night? What if I want to stay and explore more of what we started? The control. The surrender. The way you make me feel like the world narrowed to just you."

He blinks, chest rising and falling like he's fighting a battle within himself.

"Harper..."

"I just want to know if that side of you was real." My throat tightens. "And if you'd take me there again."

He's silent, but the heat in his gaze says everything his words refuse to.

I hold my breath, waiting for his next move.

Angel's Peak

Chapter 18

Caleb's eyes darken, pupils blown wide until there's barely any green left. Just black hunger. His jaw works, tendons flexing beneath skin that smells like woodsmoke and pine. Every breath he takes is measured, controlled—the way he always is when he's fighting something inside himself.

Then he steps in. Closer. Into my space. Into me. I back up. Back. Back. Back, until my boot hits the porch step. Caleb follows as the air between us thickens, charged with everything unsaid. My skin prickles with awareness as his body heat radiates across the inches that separate us.

Too much distance.

Not enough barriers.

"You want me to take control?" His voice drops into that place that turns my spine liquid, that dark register that promises things my body remembers even when my mind tries to forget. "You want me to lead?"

My heart slams against my ribs. I nod, swallow hard around the lump in my throat. "Yes. I want—"

"Then listen." His words cut through me, sharp and clean. My stomach twists with anticipation, that familiar ache starting low and deep. The air feels too thick to breathe. I'm ready to say yes to anything—to kneel, to bend, to break myself open for him again.

"You'll take the Australia assignment." He leans in, mouth brushing my ear. His breath ghosts across my skin, raising goosebumps.

The words hit like a slap.

I jerk back, stunned and stumbling. My mind reels, trying to reconcile what I thought was happening with what he just said.

"What? No—Caleb, that's not—"

"You said you want me to lead. To make the call." His voice is ice and fire. Calm on the outside, thunder underneath. The muscle in his jaw ticks—the only tell that this is costing him something. "I'm not asking. I'm telling you to go."

My lungs constrict. "I came here ready to stay. To choose *you*. And you're pushing me away?"

Pain flashes across his face—there and gone so fast I might have imagined it, but his stance doesn't waver. "I'm doing the one thing you *said* you wanted—giving you orders. Not just the ones you like. The real ones. The hard ones."

"That's bullshit." The words explode from me, sharp with betrayal. "You just don't want to take the risk. You don't want to fight for this."

Something dangerous flares in his eyes. He steps forward, all six-foot-plus of controlled power looming over me. His hands are fists at his sides like he's physically restraining himself.

"You think that's what this is? You think this doesn't cost me everything?"

Rage and hurt surge through me. I shove him. Hard. My palms connect with his chest—solid muscle that doesn't yield. "Then show me. Stop pretending you don't want me to stay and *show me*."

His control snaps.

He grabs my wrists. Slams my back against the wall hard enough to rattle picture frames. My arms are pinned above my head before I can breathe. His body crushes into mine, every inch of him pressed against me, his erection obvious through his jeans. His mouth hovers an inch from mine, breath ragged, eyes wild.

"You *really* want this, Harper?" His voice is gravel and broken glass. "You want *that* side of me?"

My breath comes in pants. Everything in me screams yes. I nod.

"No nodding. Words." His grip tightens, fingertips digging into my pulse points.

The command shoots straight to my core. I've been craving this: a man who knows what I need before I do. The one who can take me apart and put me back together stronger.

"Yes." The word comes out as a whisper.

His eyes darken further. Green swallowed by black. That last thread of restraint visibly frays.

"Then strip. Right. Now."

My pulse slams through my veins. For a heartbeat, I hesitate—old fears, old doubts rising up.

"I said now." His voice drops, quiet and lethal.

The tone brooks no argument. It's the voice of a man who expects obedience, who *demands* it. And God help me, I want to give it to him. He backs me up until I'm pressed against the door, then he opens it, ushering me inside.

My fingers tremble as I reach for my flannel. Buttons slip through holes with agonizing slowness. His eyes track every movement, burning paths across my skin before I'm exposed. The flannel hits the floor. My tank top follows, over my head in one motion, leaving me in just a bra.

"Keep going."

The rasp in his voice makes me shiver. My hands shake

harder as I work the button of my jeans. The zipper sounds obscenely loud in the charged silence. Denim slides down my legs, pooling at my feet. I step out of them, kicking them aside.

I stand before him in nothing but black lace—the set I put on this morning without consciously admitting why.

He doesn't move. Doesn't touch. Just watches with predatory stillness that makes my skin feel too tight.

"All of it."

My breath catches. This is the moment. The precipice.

I reach behind my back. Unhook my bra. Let it fall.

My nipples tighten instantly in the cool air, or maybe from the weight of his gaze. I hook my thumbs in my panties and push them down. The last scrap of fabric whispers to the floor.

I'm bare. Exposed. Vulnerable in ways that have nothing to do with nudity.

Yet, I've never felt more alive.

He leans into me slowly, deliberately like a wolf assessing prey. His heated gaze licks down my spine. Every nerve ending screams for contact.

The silence stretches, thick with tension. My skin prickles. My core clenches on emptiness.

"You thought control meant keeping you here." He stops in front of me and catches my chin with calloused fingers. Forces my eyes to his. "But real power is knowing when to *let go*. When to walk away. When to *make* someone else walk away."

His thumb brushes my bottom lip. I fight the urge to suck it into my mouth.

He steps forward. Crowds me back until cold wall meets heated skin. His clothed body presses against my nakedness— rough denim, soft cotton, hard muscle.

"And you—Harper—you would've stayed." His breath feathers across my face. "You would've twisted yourself in knots trying to be what you think I need. And six months from now, you'd wake up beside me with resentment in your eyes. You'd blame me for what you gave up. And that?" His grip on my chin tightens. "That would kill what we're building before it ever had a chance to start."

Tears prick my eyes because he's right. Because he sees me too clearly. Because he's willing to hurt us both to *save* us.

"So this is for my own good?" My voice cracks, thick with emotion and arousal.

"No." His eyes burn into mine. "If you're talking about me fucking you, that's going to be for me—to remember you during the next six months, and for you to decide if you want to return to me." His thumb traces my bottom lip. "If this is what you want... If I'm what you want, then you'll honor my wishes. Go to Australia. Think about what you want, and whether that means more of this."

"But that's not... It makes no sense."

"Not asking." He looms closer, towering over me. "This is me choosing *us* by letting you go. You'd resent staying. That resentment would *rot* everything we've started."

"Then prove it," I snap. "Show me."

A beat. Then another. His eyes darken—not with anger, but something else. Something deeper. Wreckage and want, grief and need. A storm I feel in my bones.

He closes the distance.

His mouth crashes into mine, a brutal, desperate kiss that tears the air from my lungs. This isn't softness. It's not seduction. It's obliteration. Teeth. Tongue. Hunger. He devours me like he's drowning and I'm the only breath he'll ever get.

When he pulls away, we're both gasping, chests heaving. His forehead rests against mine, our breath mingling in jagged rhythm.

"You don't get it, do you?" His voice is wrecked. "This is me loving you."

The words hit harder than any touch ever could. My knees almost buckle.

"Outside. Now."

He takes my hand and leads me into the night.

Barefoot, breathless, nerves alive, I follow. The cold bites, sharp and bracing, but I barely feel it over the wildfire under my skin. The scent of pine and woodsmoke. The silence of snow-draped forest. Moonlight turns the clearing silver, dreamlike.

The boulder behind the house waits, still warm from the day. He stops beside it, turns to face me, and cups my jaw in one broad, callused hand.

"You remember what you said... about this stone?" His voice is low, rough, vibrating through me. "What I said I wanted to do to you? Out here like this?"

Heat floods my face. My breath catches.

I nod.

His mouth curves in a wicked, knowing smile. "Yeah. You remember."

I swallow hard. My thighs press together involuntarily, breath quickening.

But then—he lets go.

Steps back.

The loss of contact makes me sway. The sharp edge of disappointment slices through my belly. Until his hands are suddenly at my waist, lifting me effortlessly onto the boulder. It's smooth against my bare skin, warmed by the sun but cooled by evening, grounding and solid beneath me.

He parts my thighs.

Kneels.

My heart stops.

"Caleb—"

"This is what you get," he says, his gaze blazing up into mine. "For now."

His hands curl around my hips like he owns them. Like he owns me. The first swipe of his tongue steals my breath.

He worships.

Not with cruelty. Not with control. But with devotion.

"If you come back—if you choose me—we'll talk about fantasies." His voice is darker now, full of promise and warning. "But this? This is what I want you to remember."

Then he leans in. Every stroke is reverent. Every growl against my skin is a benediction. I arch. I tremble. I shatter, again and again, until I'm boneless, breathless, broken open and whole in the same heartbeat.

And everything else disappears.

The trees. The stars. The night itself.

All gone.

Replaced by the heat of his mouth, the relentless rhythm of his tongue, the low growls of satisfaction vibrating against my skin. My fingers tangle in his hair. My head falls back. Every nerve lights up with need. With knowing.

I'll never forget this.

Not if I live to be a hundred.

When he rises, his lips glisten and his pupils are blown wide. He kisses me like he's never going to stop. Like maybe he never should.

Then he lifts me again, this time into his arms, cradling me like something precious. Like something he already knows he can't afford to lose.

He takes me back inside and lays me on the bed, and then...

He fucks me like he's angry. Like he's grieving. Like he's already missing me. Like he's leaving pieces of himself inside me to carry to Australia. Branding his name beneath my skin.

I meet every thrust, hands scrabbling for purchase. The wet sounds of our joining fill the air along with our ragged breathing, my whimpers, his growls.

"Remember me." His free hand finds my throat. Not squeezing, just holding. Possessing. "Remember this feeling when I'm not there."

The words break something in him.

This angle is deep. More primal. He sets a punishing rhythm that has me climbing toward release embarrassingly fast.

I whimper. Try to hold back the tide building inside me, but he knows my body too well. Knows exactly how to push me to the edge. His fingers find my clit, circling with devastating precision.

He pulls almost all the way out. Slams back in.

I shatter.

My climax rips through me like lightning, every nerve ending firing at once. I scream as my body convulses around him. He fucks me through it, prolonging the waves until I'm sobbing from overstimulation.

Only then does he let himself go. His rhythm falters. His grip tightens. He buries himself deep with a roar that sounds like my name and empties himself inside me.

When we collapse together afterward, tangled and raw, I don't feel broken. I feel *whole*.

For long moments, neither of us moves. Just harsh breathing and racing hearts, gradually slowing. His weight pins me, grounding me as I float in a state of bliss.

Eventually, he pulls out carefully. Gathers me in his arms. I curl into his chest, boneless and sated. His fingers card through my tangled hair. Lips press against my temple.

When he finally speaks, his voice is gentle. "Go to Australia." His arms tighten around me. "Chase the thing you've worked for. Prove to yourself that you can. Shine as bright as you can, and if you still want this with me—want *us* —when you come back, I'll be here. I'm not going anywhere."

I want to argue. Want to rage against the logic of it, but deep down, I know he's right.

If I stay, I'll wonder.

That *what-if* would poison us.

"I hate that you're right," I whisper against his chest.

"I know." His chest rumbles with a quiet laugh. "I hate it, too."

We don't sleep. Not really.

Instead, he makes love to me again. And again. Slow and tender, as if memorizing the exact shape of my body beneath his hands. Then harder, rougher, and frantic with the urgency of goodbye.

There are moments when we laugh breathlessly into each other's mouths, and moments when he fucks me like it's the last thing tethering him to the earth.

When the first light of dawn slips through the window, we're tangled in each other, sweat-damp and aching, skin marked with the memory of everything we didn't say.

Because today, I leave.

Angel's Peak

Chapter 19

I stand at the gate, backpack biting into my shoulders, camera case clutched like it might anchor me to something solid. Like it might stop me from unraveling.

My body still aches in the most decadent, savage ways. My body is a map of him.

Of Us.

Bruises bloom across my hips like love notes in violet and gold, his beard left my thighs tender and flushed, and every shift of my weight awakens the soreness he carved into me.

My hips are sore from how hard he held me. My thighs tremble with the ghosts of his hands, the rasp of his beard, the way his mouth dragged over my skin like he was memorizing the taste of goodbye.

I still feel the way his hand flattened across my skin, grounding me.

And lower—where he claimed me so fiercely—I ache. Still slick with the memory of him. Still swollen from being taken, again and again, until I couldn't tell where he ended and I began.

I shift again, thighs pressed together, and it hits—the pulse. The slow, throbbing reminder that I was his. That I am his, even as I board this plane and leave him behind.

God, I didn't expect it to feel like this. Like grief and glory braided together. Like walking away from fire and into shadow.

Some stupid part of me—hopeful, delusional—thought he might come. Thought maybe I'd turn and see him at the end of the corridor, arms crossed, flannel shirt open at the throat, eyes burning with the kind of need that makes men forget their reasons and chase what they want.

But he's not here.

Just ticketed passengers with suitcases and cell phones, calling out to bored children or texting people who are waiting for them on the other side.

No one is watching me with reverence. No one is imagining my skin under their hands. No one here will miss me like he will.

His voice echoes inside me—gravel and warmth, pain and purpose—all tangled into the words he whispered against my hair as sunlight slid across the cabin floor. He lives in my bones now. That final command, murmured into my hair as the sun crept across the floor of his cabin, painting us both in honey and farewell:

"Go. And come back to me whole."

I choke on the way it echoes inside me.

Fierce. Final. Unshakable.

The boarding call crackles overhead. *Final call for Sydney.*

I should move. Instead, I breathe.

My feet don't obey. Not at first. Because leaving doesn't feel triumphant—it feels like peeling off skin. Like walking away from warmth into an endless wind.

Still, I do what he told me.

I shoulder my bag. Step forward. Take my place in line.

Sometimes love isn't about staying.

Sometimes love is letting go... and trusting what comes back.

Inside, the plane is freezing. A frigid, sterile cold, different from the mountain wind. It creeps through steel and fiberglass and into my spine, but it doesn't numb me. Nothing could—not after the way he touched me. Not after the way he made me feel.

I sink into my seat, tugging my hoodie over my head. I close my eyes and pretend I'm breathing him in—pine, smoke, sweat, sex.

Once we're in the air, I keep my window shades down. I feel the vastness of the sky just beyond them and the distance stretching between me and the only man who's ever seen me, not just with eyes, but with soul-deep certainty. I don't have to see it to make it feel real.

The air in the cabin smells like recycled nothing, but I swear I can still catch pine sap and firewood, and the scent of his flannel tangled in my hair.

I press my forehead to the window and breathe.

Australia hits like a punch to the senses.

Jet lag clings to me like a second skin. The air in Sydney is thick and hot, tinged with eucalyptus, dust, and a faint metallic scent in the soil.

The sun is relentless. The heat has teeth, and the humidity crawls along my skin like invisible fingers. Everything feels louder here—the calls of magpies echoing like laughter, car horns sharper and more urgent, cicadas drone like static turned up too loud, and even the rustle of the leaves sounds like whispers I can't quite decipher.

The colors here are all wrong and utterly perfect—deep rusts, sun-bleached greens, birds in shades that belong in paintings, not real life. It's a photographer's dream, but I can't enjoy it.

The first days are a blur. Jet lag clings to me. I hike through scrubland with my camera strapped across my chest like armor. The locals are kind but distant.

I don't blame them—I'm brittle. Quiet.

Distant in ways I don't yet have a language for.

But I'm shooting. Constantly.

And something *is* different.

I can't describe it, except to say *the work flows.*

My hands are steady. My eye is clear. There's a sharpness in how I frame each shot—a rawness I couldn't access before.

Everything inside me is cracked open and pouring out into the lens. Shaping each shot into magic.

I send in my first batch of photos to my editor.

The email pings two hours later: *"These are phenomenal. Are you possessed?"*

I smile.

No. Not possessed.

Caleb and I speak when we can. Time zones and terrain conspire against us, but when his name lights up my screen, it's like there's breath in my lungs again.

The first time he calls, I'm crouched in the shadow of a bluff, camera balanced on my knee, waiting for a flock of galahs to burst into flight. My phone buzzes, the screen lights up with his name, and I forget how to breathe.

"Hey," I whisper, throat raw with longing.

"Hi, sweetheart." His voice is low and warm, a velvet rasp that slides over every frayed edge inside me. "You all right?"

The question is simple. The answer is not.

I swallow. "I don't know. Everything smells like salt and sunshine, and I hate how much I wish it smelled like smoke and pine."

He's quiet for a beat. Then, "What do you see?"

I glance through the lens. "A hundred pink birds about to take flight. The sky's gold. And I'm aching for you."

His inhale is sharp. "I knew you'd make something beautiful out there. But fuck, I miss you."

"Say it again."

He doesn't ask what I mean. "I miss you. I think about you every damn night. About that look in your eyes when you kneel for me and how you gasp when I make you come."

My thighs clench. I press my lips together to keep quiet. There are people nearby.

He chuckles. Low. Dirty. "You wet for me already?"

"Always."

"Good. Stay wet. Remember exactly how it felt when I told you what to do. When I bent you over and—"

The call drops. Static. Then silence.

I stare at the blank screen. My heart clenches.

But I'm smiling. Because even that—*especially* that—is more than I ever thought I'd have.

Sometimes the calls are brief. Just a few seconds of his voice and a shitty connection before it drops. Sometimes they're long, filled with stories, longing, and heat.

Once, he says, "Tell me what you're wearing."

And I do.

Another time, I ask what he sees out the cabin window.

He says, "That boulder."

I press my thighs together and close my eyes.

———

Weeks pass, then months. The land imprints itself on me slowly, like a lover with rough hands. Dust settles into my boots. The sun peels my shoulders raw. The wind carries stories I don't understand, but I hear its rhythm.

I wake before dawn, hike until my calves scream, crouch behind boulders, or cling to tree limbs, all to get the perfect shot. The camera becomes my voice, and in the still moments between clicks, I think about Caleb. About the weight of his hand. The gravity of his voice.

And the love I didn't know I could have.

The ache in my chest doesn't fade, but it becomes something I carry like my camera—ever-present, always ready.

I send in a portfolio. My editor calls the next day.

"Harper, these are... Jesus. These are national feature-level. What the hell happened to you out there?"

I lean against the tent pole and look at the sky.

"I remembered who I am."

"Well, National Geographic agrees." My editor practically screams. *"They confirmed the feature. You've outdone yourself."*

I should be ecstatic. And I am—part of me. But there's this empty place inside me, and it pulses with one name.

"I've got another offer," my editor says. *"Intimate series. Local angles. Interviews, photojournalism. They want you."*

"I'm not staying in Australia," I say flatly.

"It's not in Australia."

I still. The silence between us stretches.

"It's in Colorado," he continues. *"Angel's Peak. It's about conservation. Rangers. Poaching prevention. Threatened species. Real heart stuff. Your kind of story."*

"Angel's Peak?" My pulse trips. My breath leaves me. He keeps talking, but I barely hear him. My heartbeat is in my throat. "Did you say Angel's Peak?"

"Yeah. Real earthy, intimate stuff. I thought of you immediately. You're already familiar with the area."

I close my eyes and remember the heat of Caleb's body, the grip of his hands, the sound of his voice whispering, *Come back to me.*

Angel's Peak. The mountains. The forest.

Caleb

I look down at my hands—callused, sun-darkened, strong.

He was right all along. If I stayed... I never would have accomplished this: a feature article in National Geographic. I never would've known what I was capable of. I would've regretted not taking the challenge.

And it's time.

I'm ready to go home.

Angel's Peak

Chapter 20

The plane lands with a jolt that rattles my bones, sending a cascade of shivers up my spine. My fingers grip the armrests until my knuckles turn white. The seatbelt sign dings off, and every passenger leaps for their overhead compartments like the last chopper out of a war zone.

I move slower. My limbs are lead, but my pulse is a wildfire raging beneath my skin, threatening to consume me from the inside out.

Six months. It's been six months since I left this place. Left him. The thought sends another tremor through me. What if things are different? What if he's changed? What if I've changed?

Can we rekindle the spark?

The customs officer's voice barely registers. His questions float past me like debris in a current. My answers are automatic, rehearsed. My mind is elsewhere—already racing through the terminal, already in his arms. One thought pounds in rhythm with my heart—*he's here.*

When I step through the sliding doors into baggage claim, the wall of noise hits me first. Reunions are in full swing, voices calling out, squeals of delight, the metallic whine of the carousel. I scan the crowd, eyes darting frantically between faces. For a second, my heart stalls completely.

Strangers.

So many unfamiliar faces blur together under harsh fluorescent lights, making my eyes water.

And then—I see him.

Flannel shirt, the color of forest shadows. Faded jeans worn thin at the knees. That steel-cut jaw I've traced a thousand times with my fingertips in my dreams. Green eyes—the exact shade of the mountain pines in sunlight—locked on mine like he's been staring at this spot for hours, willing me to materialize from thin air.

He drops the cardboard sign he's holding. My name in his handwriting crumples to the floor. He doesn't even wait for the crowd to part.

He moves toward me. Steady. Inevitable.

I run to him, my feet slamming the linoleum, my breath burning in my lungs like wildfire and smoke. We collide in the center of the terminal like something torn from a fever dream.

His arms crush me to his chest with a force that would hurt if it wasn't exactly what I've been starving for. My legs wrap around his waist on pure instinct. I bury my face in his neck, inhaling the scent of pine and woodsmoke and *him*— Caleb, my Caleb—and he lifts me, *spins me*, in a wide, dizzying circle that makes me laugh and sob simultaneously.

His voice is in my ear, low and choked and everything I've replayed in my dreams.

"God, I missed you." The words vibrate against my skin.

"I missed you so much," I whisper back, my lips brushing the stubble on his jaw, feeling each coarse hair against my sensitive skin. "Every second."

When he sets me down, his calloused hands frame my face

like I'm made of glass. His eyes are wet, glistening like river stones. His kiss is brutal.

Desperate.

Months of absence poured into the slide of lips, the clash of teeth, the low groan rumbling from his chest when my tongue meets his. He tastes like coffee, and mint, and coming home.

"I need you in my truck. Now," he rasps against my mouth, his breath hot and ragged.

"Yes." I kiss him again, harder this time, claiming. "Take me home."

The ride up the mountain is silence, and heat, and anticipation thick enough to choke on. His hand never leaves my thigh, a brand through my jeans. His thumb draws slow, scorching circles just above my knee, each sweep inching higher. I shift in the seat, thighs inching farther apart of their own accord, and he groans—a primal sound that reverberates through the cab.

"Harper..." My name in his mouth is a warning, a prayer.

"Touch me." The words escape, raw with need.

"Not until I get you alone." His voice is gravel and promise. "Not until I can take my time."

He takes the corners sharp, tires spitting gravel, like he's racing the need clawing up both our spines. Every glance from him is molten copper, burning through my defenses. My body is already soaked, every nerve ending trained on him, on *what comes next*.

Six months of fantasies are about to become reality.

The forest thickens around us, familiar yet somehow more vibrant than I remember. Sunlight filters through pine needles, casting dappled shadows across the dashboard. The scent of mountain air fills the cab each time Caleb cracks his window—crisp, clean, carrying the hope of endless nights under stars and mornings wrapped in quilts on the porch.

When we pull up in front of the cabin—*our* cabin, though I never let myself call it that before—we don't even make it to the door.

His hand is on my ass the moment I step from the truck, pulling me flush against him. My backpack hits the ground with a dull thud. He's kissing me like possession, like worship. I tear at his shirt buttons, desperate to reach skin. He yanks mine over my head in one fluid motion, cold air raising goosebumps across my exposed flesh.

The door slams open beneath his shoulder, and we tumble inside. Heat explodes between us, six months of restraint evaporating like morning mist.

His mouth blazes a trail down my throat, my collarbones, the swell of my breasts above my bra. My hands tangle in his hair—longer now, wild, pulling, begging without words. He lifts me like I weigh nothing, and I wrap around him again, breathless as he lays me out across the wooden table where we shared our meals.

"Fuck, I need you," he growls, fingers hooking into my jeans, peeling them down my legs like he's unwrapping something precious. "I dreamed about this. Every goddamn night."

The reverence in his eyes as he looks down at me, laid bare and vulnerable, makes my chest ache with everything unspoken between us.

His mouth crashes into mine like a wave against cliffs. One hand tangles in my hair, tugging just enough to make my back arch. The other cups my face like I'm something fragile, even as he's taking me apart piece by piece with each burning touch.

He doesn't tease. Doesn't wait.

He drives into me with a growl that vibrates through my bones, filling me in one hard, perfect stroke that makes me scream his name into the cabin's hushed air. My body stretches, accommodates, and welcomes him home.

We move like we never left each other. Like time bent to

our will. Like the mountain waited too, holding its breath for my return. Every thrust is a confession. Every gasp is a promise kept.

"Caleb," I gasp, nails dragging down his back, leaving trails of crimson in their wake. "Harder. I need to feel you."

His fingers dig into my hips, lifting me slightly, slamming deeper. "Say it." His voice is strained, desperate. "Say what you couldn't before you left."

"I love you," I choke out, the truth breaking free after months of denial. "God, I love you."

He stills. Just for a breath. Just long enough for the words to settle between us like a promise.

"I love you, too." Then he kisses me like he's dying and I'm oxygen.

The words break something wide open. Inside both of us. Something that had been locked away, festering.

He flips me with gentle force, bends me over the table. One hand slides into my hair, tightening just enough to make me gasp, to make my back bow.

"You still want my control?" His breath is hot against my ear.

"Yes." No hesitation. No fear.

Then he's inside me again, fucking me until I'm raw with it, ruined and rebuilt in the span of heartbeats. His rhythm is relentless, each thrust driving me higher, closer to that precipice. His fingers find me where we're joined, circling, pressing, demanding my surrender.

"Come for me," he commands, voice wrecked. "Let me feel you."

My release crashes through me like a tsunami, vision blurring at the edges, muscles clenching around him as he follows me over, his body shuddering against mine, within mine.

Until there's nothing left of the months we spent apart— only the now. Only the fire. Only him.

When we collapse in a heap on the floor, tangled in half-shed clothes and breathless kisses, he gathers me into his arms, presses his mouth to my temple where my pulse still races beneath thin skin.

"You came back." Wonder and fear mingle in his voice, as if I might dissolve into mountain mist.

"I came home," I correct him.

Angel's Peak

CHAPTER 21

EPILOGUE: ONE YEAR LATER

"Hold still, you ridiculous bird." I adjust my telephoto lens, tracking the northern goshawk perched regally on a dead pine. The morning light bathes its sleek feathers in golden warmth, transforming ordinary gray to luminous silver. "Just one more second..."

The bird, predictably, ignores my whispered plea, launching into flight just as I press the shutter. I capture its departure anyway—wings extended, powerful and graceful against the backdrop of endless Colorado sky.

"Got it?" Caleb's voice carries from inside the cabin, followed by the scent of fresh coffee wafting through the open door.

"Got something." I lower my camera, rolling stiff shoulders as I turn toward the sound. "Maybe not the portrait I wanted, but possibly better."

The deck where I stand—a new addition to the once-modest cabin—offers a panoramic view of the valley, morning mist still clinging to distant ridges. Bird feeders hang from the eaves, attracting a colorful array of mountain chickadees and nuthatches that have become regular subjects of my more casual photography.

I gather my equipment, moving carefully to accommodate the pronounced curve of my seven-month pregnant belly. The nursery addition to the cabin is nearly complete, its fresh pine walls visible around the corner of the main structure. Caleb has spent every free weekend for months crafting built-in furniture, installing windows positioned to capture morning light, creating a perfect space for the child we hadn't planned but now can't imagine our lives without.

Inside, the cabin has transformed as much as our lives have. The spartan bachelor quarters I first encountered have evolved into a true home—still neat but lived-in, with my photography equipment sharing space with Caleb's research materials, colorful throws softening practical furniture, walls adorned with framed prints of my work alongside maps of the wilderness we both cherish.

Caleb stands at the stove, spatula in hand, the domesticity of the scene still occasionally surprising me after years of solitary hotel rooms and temporary accommodations.

"Perfect timing." He slides a vegetable omelet onto a plate. "Breakfast is ready."

"Smells amazing." I set my camera on its designated shelf—organization being one of our earliest and most necessary compromises—before joining him at the table.

He places a hand on my rounded belly, wonder still evident in his expression whenever he feels the life growing within me. "How's Junior this morning?"

"Active. Very active." I cover his hand with mine. "Apparently planning to be a soccer player or possibly a kickboxer."

His smile—still capable of accelerating my heartbeat after a year together—warms his entire face. "Takes after his mother. Never stops moving."

"His? What if *he's* a she?"

"I'd love that." Caleb can't contain his excitement. "Boy or girl, I couldn't be happier."

"Speaking of which." I take a bite of the omelet, humming appreciation. "The conservation board called yesterday while you were in town. They've approved funding for the expanded survey."

Pride flashes in his eyes. "They'd be fools not to. Your first year's documentation has already led to three new protected areas."

The Achievement in Conservation Photography award sitting on our mantle validates his assessment. The series of images I captured over the past year—from golden eagles to nearly invisible lynx, from spring wildflower explosions to winter's pristine stillness—has resonated beyond our expectations, bringing national attention to Angel's Peak's ecological significance.

"It's not just the photographs." I reach for his hand across the table. "Your ecological context makes them meaningful. The conservation workshops you've developed have turned awareness into action."

He shrugs, still uncomfortable with praise despite the remarkable evolution of the past year. The reclusive ranger has become a respected educator, splitting his time between field-work and teaching local students about forest stewardship. The walls he maintained for so long have gradually lowered, allowing his natural passion for this wilderness to inspire others.

"The school group yesterday asked when you'd be coming back." He changes the subject, but the pleased flush coloring his cheeks betrays his satisfaction. "Apparently, my explanations of wildlife photography techniques don't compare to the real thing."

"Next week, after the doctor's appointment." I rest a hand

on my belly. "While I can still move without waddling too obviously."

"You don't waddle." His straight-faced delivery makes me laugh.

"Liar. Very sweet liar." I rise to clear our plates, dropping a kiss on his head as I pass. "But I appreciate the effort."

"Almost forgot." He catches my hand, keeping me close. "Happy anniversary."

The simple words send warmth cascading through me. One year since I officially moved into the cabin. One year of building this life that neither of us had imagined possible when a storm first threw us together.

"I have something planned." His eyes hold mischief rarely seen by others. "If you're up for a short hike."

"To our spot?" Anticipation quickens my pulse.

The trail to "our spot"—the overlook where I captured the perfect eagle shot and where, later, we made our first tentative commitment to a shared future—has become a familiar path. We travel it in all seasons now: summer's vibrant greenery, autumn's spectacular color transformation, winter's pristine snowscape, and now spring's renewed awakening.

Today, wildflowers carpet the forest floor, trillium and columbine creating patches of color amid unfurling ferns. Caleb walks beside me, pace adjusted to my slower, pregnancy-altered gait, one hand resting protectively at the small of my back on steeper sections.

"Remember how you basically sprinted up this trail the first time?" His teasing carries affection rather than mockery. "Desperate to get your eagle shot before the storm hit."

"And you, grumpy mountain man, kept sighing loudly every time I stopped to photograph something." I nudge his ribs playfully.

"I wasn't grumpy." His protest carries no conviction. "I was... focused."

"Focused on being grumpy." I capture his mock outrage with a quick camera snap, adding to my extensive collection of "Caleb expressions" that has grown throughout our year together.

The overlook, when we reach it, remains as breathtaking as ever—the vast panorama of mountains stretching to impossible horizons, valleys lush with spring growth, the distant silver thread of rivers catching sunlight. Caleb spreads a blanket on our usual boulder, helping me settle before retrieving something from his backpack.

"I have something for you." He hands me a wrapped package, uncharacteristic nervousness flickering across his features.

The simple brown paper falls away to reveal a handcrafted wooden box. Its surface is inlaid with a delicate pattern of mountain ridges and soaring birds. The craftsmanship showcases his woodworking craft.

"Caleb, it's beautiful." My fingers trace the intricate design, recognizing the distinctive silhouette of a golden eagle among the inlaid birds.

"Open it." He sits beside me, anticipation evident in his posture.

Inside, nestled on velvet lining, lies a leather-bound book. My breath catches as I lift it, recognizing the title embossed in simple gold lettering: "Convergence: A Year in Angel's Peak."

"You made this?" I open the cover with reverent fingers, discovering page after page of my photographs arranged in unexpected pairings—wildlife portraits alongside human moments, macro details of forest flora beside sweeping landscapes, all telling the story of the past year.

"I selected the images." His arm slides around my waist, anchoring me against him. "A professional did the binding. But the concept... I wanted to show how our separate paths became one. How this place brought us together."

I turn pages slowly; each spread revealing thoughtful

juxtapositions—the golden eagle soaring above the ridge paired with a candid shot of Caleb teaching students beside a similar overlook. A close-up of fox kits playing near their den alongside a stolen shot of Caleb asleep on the couch, peaceful vulnerability evident in both images.

"These are from my personal collection." I recognize photographs never intended for publication—intimate moments captured for my eyes only. "How did you get them?"

"Your backup drive isn't as securely password-protected as you might think." The admission carries no apology, only quiet satisfaction. "And you're not the only one who can be sneaky with a camera."

Indeed, several images show me unaware of being photographed—focused on adjusting equipment, watching wildlife with unguarded wonder, even one particularly enormous shot of me sleeping, hair wild across the pillow, that makes me laugh out loud.

"Revenge photography?" I raise an eyebrow, unable to summon genuine indignation.

"Documentation." He tucks a strand of hair behind my ear, his touch lingering against my cheek. "Important scientific record."

As I near the end of the book, one page steals my breath entirely—our ultrasound image, the grainy profile of our child in utero, placed beside a photograph of the golden eagle's nest with barely visible eaglets huddled within. New life, sheltered and precious, in perfect parallel.

The final page holds text rather than images, handwritten in Caleb's precise script:

Some journeys bring us to destinations we never knew we were seeking. Some storms lead to shelters that become homes. Some chance encounters become the photographs we frame our lives around. Thank you for staying when you could have gone. For turning my sanctuary into our home.

All my love, always, C.

Tears blur my vision, pregnancy hormones amplifying already powerful emotions. "This is the most beautiful gift I've ever received."

His arms encircle me, his chin resting on my shoulder as we gaze together at the panorama before us. "I wanted to mark this year properly. Everything changed when you showed up at my door."

"For the better?" I lean into his embrace, still occasionally needing reassurance that this settled life hasn't diminished him as my traveling one hasn't diminished me.

"Beyond better." His hand splays protectively over our growing child. "I never imagined adding a third ranger to our station quite so soon."

"Ranger?" I twist to see his face. "I thought we were raising a wildlife photographer."

"Clearly both." The compromise comes easily, part of our ongoing playful negotiation about our child's future. "A photographing ranger. Or a ranging photographer."

"We have time to figure it out." I settle against him, contentment seeping through me like the warm spring sunshine. "Though we should probably figure out an actual name before 'Junior' sticks permanently."

"I've been thinking about that." His voice carries the careful consideration he brings to all important matters. "What about Aspen for a girl? Or River for a boy?"

"Nature names." I smile, unsurprised by his preference. "I like them."

"And Kim or James as middle names." He offers this more hesitantly. "After your father and..."

"After two people who loved this wilderness and taught us to see it clearly." I cover his hand with mine, deeply touched by the suggestion. "Perfect."

A shadow passes overhead—large, distinctive in its soaring

pattern. We both look up, recognizing the golden eagle that has become so familiar over the past year, its territory encompassing the ridge where we sit.

"Still here." Pride colors Caleb's voice. "The anti-poaching initiatives are working."

"The educational programs help too." I raise my camera instinctively, capturing the magnificent bird against the limitless blue. "Hard to harm what you've learned to love."

We've both found what we needed in this unexpected partnership—for me, a home that doesn't constrain but anchors, allowing my work to gain depth through sustained observation; for Caleb, connection that enhances rather than threatens his devotion to this wilderness, his purpose expanded by sharing it with others.

"I've been thinking." I lower my camera, turning to face him fully. "After the baby comes, once we're settled into a routine... what would you think about expanding the documentation project?"

His eyebrow raises in silent question.

"The Yellowstone ecosystem faces similar pressures. They're looking for a comprehensive visual record combined with community education." Excitement builds as I outline the idea that's been forming for months. "Three weeks there, maybe four times a year. You could develop conservation workshops for their rangers, and I could extend the documentation methodology we've created here. We could take the baby, start their education early."

Rather than hesitation, his face shows thoughtful consideration. "Family field research."

"Exactly." I watch his expression, seeing not reluctance but practical assessment. "We'd maintain a home base here, but expand our impact."

"Our next adventure." His smile confirms what I already

knew—that the man who once feared connection now embraces it as strengthening rather than limiting. "I like it."

As the sun descends toward distant peaks, we gather our things, preparing for the return journey. Caleb carefully repacks the precious book, helping me rise from our stone seat with gentle hands. The trail ahead leads back to our expanded cabin, the nursery awaiting its occupant, and the life we've built from storm and circumstance.

At the overlook's edge, we pause for one final look at the wilderness that brought us together—not through random chance, as I once believed, but through parallel devotion to something larger than ourselves. The golden eagle circles once more before disappearing beyond the ridge, returning to its mate and growing young.

"Ready?" Caleb's hand finds mine, warm and solid and real.

"Ready." I lace my fingers through his, certainty flowing through me.

Tomorrow brings a doctor's appointment in town, then a school presentation, and then continued work on documentation that may help preserve this landscape beyond our lifetimes. Next month brings our child, and next year, perhaps new territories to explore together. The path ahead holds challenges alongside joy, compromise alongside adventure.

Standing at the threshold between wilderness and home, between past and future, our child moves between us—a decisive kick that makes us both laugh. Caleb's arms wrap around me as our child kicks between us.

After a lifetime of capturing moments, I've finally found the one I want to live in forever.

LOVE THE HEAT IN ANGEL'S PEAK?

If you're enjoying all the steamy, small-town instalove stories this mountain town has to offer, you're going to fall hard for Snowbound with the Vineyard Owner.

This next swoon-worthy romance serves up spice, sweetness, and a hero who knows exactly what he wants—*her*.

➡ Click here to dive into Snowbound with the Vineyard Owner

When a blizzard traps a high-powered sommelier with a brooding mountain winemaker, sparks fly hotter than mulled wine by the fire 🔥

Elena Santiago's career is hanging by a thread after her ex stole credit for her work. Her last chance? Securing exclusive rights to Colorado's most elusive vineyard. But when a snowstorm sends her car sliding off a mountain road, she finds herself stranded with Dominic Mercer—the reclusive vintner she came to woo.

Dominic has spent five years hiding on his mountain, crafting extraordinary wines while nursing wounds from a tragic fire that destroyed everything. The last thing he needs is a sharp-tongued California critic invading his sanctuary... especially one whose midnight-dark eyes see straight through his carefully constructed walls.

Trapped together in his remote vineyard, professional boundaries blur as fast as the snow falls. Elena's expertise challenges everything Dominic thought he knew about wine, while his passionate intensity awakens desires she's kept buried beneath ambition. But with only one bed and three days until rescue, their enemies-to-lovers dance becomes impossible to resist.

When the roads clear, will Elena choose the career that's betrayed her... or the mountain man who's stolen her heart?

Perfect for fans of:

Grumpy-sunshine romance

Forced proximity

Workplace rivals to lovers

Snowed in/one bed

Boss babe meets mountain man

Instalove with sizzling steam

Some storms change everything. Some risks are worth taking. Some blends are absolutely perfect.

Click here to dive into Snowbound with the Vineyard Owner

Catch up on the Angel's Peak Small Town Instalove Romance Series Featuring the TROPES you LOVE

FORCED PROXIMITY - STRANDED TOGETHER during mountain storms

Grumpy/Sunshine - Brooding ranger meets spirited photographer

Wounded Hero - Haunted by tragic past, rebuilt by love

Instalove - Instant attraction that deepens into forever love

Wilderness Romance - Passion ignites in pristine mountain setting

Opposites Attract - Nomadic adventurer vs. rooted protector

Alpha Hero - Dominant, protective, utterly devoted

🔥 Steamy Romance - Explosive chemistry and passionate encounters

💕 Found Family - Building home together in the wilderness

📷 Career vs Love - Choosing between dreams and destiny

🦅 Shared Purpose - Wildlife conservation brings them together

🏡 Home is Where the Heart Is - Finding belonging in unexpected places

Angel's Peak

PLEASE CONSIDER LEAVING A REVIEW

I HOPE YOU ENJOYED THIS BOOK AS MUCH AS I enjoyed writing it. If you like this book, please leave a review. I love reviews. I love reading your reviews, and they help other readers decide if this book is worth their time and money. I hope you think it is and decide to share this story with others. A sentence is all it takes. Thank you in advance!

Angel's Peak

ELLZ BELLZ

Ellie's Facebook Reader Group

If you are interested in joining the ELLZ BELLZ, Ellie's Facebook reader group, we'd love to have you.

Join Ellie's ELLZ BELLZ.
The ELLZ BELLZ Facebook Reader Group

Sign up for Ellie's Newsletter.
Elliemasters.com/newslettersignup

Rescuing Malia

Rescuing Ally (Part 1)

Rescuing Ally (Part 2)

Delta Team

Rescuing Ember

Rescuing Aria

STANDALONES IN THE GUARDIAN HOSTAGE RESCUE SERIES YOU CAN READ ANYTIME

Military Romance

Guardian Personal Protection Specialists

Sybil's Protector

Lyra's Protector

Angel's Peak Series

Steamy Instalove Small Town

EACH BOOK IN THIS SERIES CAN BE READ AS A STANDALONE AND IS ABOUT A DIFFERENT COUPLE WITH AN HEA.

SNOWED IN WITH THE MOUNTAIN DOCTOR

Rescued by the Mountain Guide

Stranded with the Resort Owner

Matched with the Small-Town Chef

Trapped with the Forest Ranger

Snowbound with the Vineyard Owner

Reunited with the Hometown Hero

Colliding with the Coffee Shop Owner

Falling for the Firefighter

Wrecked with the Reclusive Author

Tangled with the Single Dad

Whirlwinded by the Helicopter Pilot

Sheltered by the Veterinarian

Bound by the Sheriff

The One I Want Series

(Small Town, Military Heroes)

By Jet & Ellie Masters

EACH BOOK IN THIS SERIES CAN BE READ AS A STANDALONE AND IS ABOUT A DIFFERENT COUPLE WITH AN HEA.

Saving Abby

Saving Ariel

Saving Brie

Saving Cate

Saving Dani

Saving Jen

The LaRouge Triplets

Asher

Brody

Cage

Billionaire Romance

Billionaire Boys Club

Hawke

Richard

Contemporary Romance

Cocky Captain

About the Author

Ellie Masters is a USA Today Bestselling author and Amazon Top 15 Author who writes Angsty, Steamy, Heart-Stopping, Pulse-Pounding, Can't-Stop-Reading Romantic Suspense. In addition, she's a wife, military mom, doctor, and retired Colonel. She writes romantic suspense filled with all your sexy, swoon-worthy alpha men. Her writing will tug at your heart-strings and leave your heart racing.

Born in the South, raised under the Hawaiian sun, Ellie has traveled the globe while in service to her country. The love of her life, her amazing husband, is her number one fan and biggest supporter. And yes! He's read every word she's written.

She has lived all over the United States—east, west, north, south and central—but grew up under the Hawaiian sun. She's also been privileged to have lived overseas, experiencing other cultures and making lifelong friends. Now, Ellie is proud to call herself a Southern transplant, learning to say y'all and "bless her heart" with the best of them.

Ellie's favorite way to spend an evening is curled up on a couch, laptop in place, watching a fire, drinking a good wine, and bringing forth all the characters from her mind to the page and hopefully into the hearts of her readers.

FOR MORE INFORMATION
elliemasters.com

facebook.com/elliemastersromance

x.com/Ellie__Masters

instagram.com/ellie_masters

bookbub.com/authors/ellie-masters

goodreads.com/Ellie_Masters

Connect with Ellie Masters

Website:
elliemasters.com
Purchase Direct:
elliemasters.com/shopify
Amazon Author Page:
elliemasters.com/amazon
Facebook:
elliemasters.com/Facebook
Goodreads:
elliemasters.com/Goodreads
Bookbub:
elliemasters.com/Bookbub
Instagram:
elliemasters.com/Instagram

Final Thoughts

I hope you enjoyed this book as much as I enjoyed writing it. If you enjoyed reading this story, please consider leaving a review on Amazon and Goodreads, and please let other people know. A sentence is all it takes. Friend recommendations are the strongest catalyst for readers' purchase decisions! And I'd love to be able to continue bringing the characters and stories from My-Mind-to-the-Page.

Second, call or e-mail a friend and tell them about this book. If you really want them to read it, gift it to them. If you prefer digital friends, please use the "Recommend" feature of Goodreads to spread the word.

Or visit my blog https://elliemasters.com, where you can find out more about my writing process and personal life.

Come visit The EDGE: Dark Discussions where we'll have a chance to talk about my works, their creation, and maybe what the future has in store for my writing.

Facebook Reader Group: Ellz Bellz

Thank you so much for your support!

Love,

Ellie

Dedication

This book is dedicated to you, my reader. Thank you for spending a few hours of your time with me. I wouldn't be able to write without you to cheer me on. Your wonderful words, your support, and your willingness to join me on this journey is a gift beyond measure.

Whether this is the first book of mine you've read, or if you've been with me since the very beginning, thank you for believing in me as I bring these characters 'from my mind to the page and into your hearts.'

Love,
Ellie

THE END

www.ingramcontent.com/pod-product-compliance
Lightning Source LLC
Chambersburg PA
CBHW031029310726
48969CB00007B/1916